"I know I promised I wouldn't try anything, but…" Damien trailed off, as he drew his lips across Niveah's cheek, her ear and her neck "…I can't control myself when I'm around you."

Niveah didn't know how much more of this she could take. It was just a matter of time before she was gasping for air and her legs gave way. Damien cupped her chin and kissed her so fully, so passionately, Niveah felt like she was spinning on a carousel. Her shoes fell off, her dress sailed down her hips and her fifty-dollar nylons lay in pieces on the floor.

Still kissing, they stumbled farther into the suite, knocking into end tables, couch legs and other furniture. Down to just her panties, her body throbbing with heat and desire, she dragged her fingernails up his chest, across his neck and over his head. Moving to an inaudible beat, Niveah rocked her hips against his crotch, causing Damien to release a savage groan. Niveah reached around, unzipped his pants and reached inside.

"Where's your bedroo

D0818586

Books by Pamela Yaye

Kimani Romance

Other People's Business
The Trouble with Luv'
Her Kind of Man
Love TKO
Games of the Heart
Love on the Rocks
Pleasure for Two
Promises We Make

PAMELA YAYE

has a bachelor's degree in Christian education and has been writing short stories since elementary school. Her love for African-American fiction and literature prompted her to actively pursue a career in writing romance. When she's not reading or working on her latest novel, she's watching basketball, cooking or planning her next vacation. Pamela lives in Calgary, Canada, with her handsome husband, adorable daughter and precious son.

Promises We Make

PAMELA YAYE

TM
KIMANI
ROMANCE

Dedicated to my son in heaven, Justice, and my children here on earth, Aysiah and Christian. Mommy loves you very much—more than words can ever truly express.

 KIMANI PRESS™

Recycling programs for this product may not exist in your area.

ISBN-13: 978-0-373-86199-6

PROMISES WE MAKE

Copyright © 2011 by Pamela Sadadi

www.kimanipress.com

Printed in U.S.A.

Dear Reader,

What could be more salacious than a sexy office romance featuring two headstrong characters vying for the same position? While writing this story about discovering love in the workplace, I quickly realized that Niveah Evans and Damien Hunter had *much* bigger problems than just being coworkers. Their love-hate relationship is tumultuous and passionate, and the more they try to resist each other, the hotter the fire burns!

Before they can ride off into the sunset together, Damien will have to convince Niveah that his feelings for her are real. It won't be any easy task, but Damien won't stop until they have their happy ending.

My next Kimani romance novel, *Escape to Paradise* (July 2011), is a story filled with secrets, betrayal and a hero so sensitive and romantic and alpha, he'll make you swoon. To find out more about me and my novels, drop me a line at pamelayaye@aol.com or visit me at www.pamelayaye.com.

With love,

Pamela Yaye

I couldn't have asked for a better family, and feel incredibly blessed to have the following people in my life: Jean-Claude, Aysiah, and Christian Yaye. My parents, Daniel and Gwendolyn Odidison. My siblings, Kenneth and Bettey Odidison. You all mean the world to me and I love you guys something fierce!!!

Special thanks to Delly Dyer for answering my questions about the advertising/marketing business. The information you provided was invaluable and helped to improve the novel.

Chapter 1

"Is it just me or do all the men up in here look like broke-down versions of Boris Kodjoe?"

Niveah Evans laughed out loud at her best friend's assessment of the male guests at the Ritz-Carlton's annual New Year's Eve bash. Tickets to the black tie event had set her back a hundred dollars, and as she glanced around the elaborately decorated ballroom, she wondered what all the hype was about. Champagne flowed from a gold fountain and the performers suspended from the ceiling were giving one hell of a show, but it was nothing Niveah hadn't seen before. As a creative director for the largest advertising company in the U.S., it was her job to be up on the latest trends, and she'd seen the act six months earlier in a Paris nightclub.

"I can't believe no one's asked us to dance," Roxi Gonzalez complained, wrinkling her nose as if she'd just gotten a whiff of an old shoe. "I wasted the entire morning getting plucked, waxed and shaved and no one in here gives a damn."

Jeanette Miller released a deep, pitiful sigh. "This is turning out to be the worst New Year's Eve on record. I should have stayed home and watched the ball drop in Times Square."

"You're right, this is pretty bad," Niveah conceded, reaching for her mai tai, "but at least your boss isn't bringing in some clown from head office to babysit you for the next few weeks. I single-handedly landed that Discreet Boutique account, and now Mr. Russo thinks I need help. How am I supposed to shine with another creative director breathing down my neck? I have half a mind to complain to—"

Her friends groaned.

"The next time you mention your job I'm out of here," Roxi threatened, leveling a finger at her. "I came down here to have a good time, not listen to you bitch about work."

Jeanette put down her wine flute. "Niveah, you know what your problem is? Your life has no balance. All you care about is impressing Mr. Russo and getting another raise."

"What are you talking about? I travel—"

"For work," Jeanette chirped.

"I entertain on a regular basis—"

"For work."

"And I take the last Friday of every month off to recharge."

"Yeah, but that's because Mr. Russo forces you to!"

It was times like this that Niveah wished she hadn't befriended Jeanette at the company picnic five years earlier. Within weeks of meeting, they were working out together, gossiping about their colleagues and planning the first of many Las Vegas shopping trips.

Intent on being heard, Jeanette raised her voice above the rock song playing. "Working sixty hours a week is prematurely aging you. I didn't want to say anything because you just celebrated your birthday, but you've lost your youth, your shine, that healthy glow I always envied."

"You're so busy clawing your way up the corporate

ladder you don't realize that life is passing you by," Roxi continued. "You're working like a dog to forget what happened with—"

Niveah silenced her with a look. "Don't even *think* about mentioning that jerk's name. I've moved on, and I wish you guys would, too."

"We will, as soon as you start living again." Smiling sympathetically, Jeanette rested a hand on her best friend's shoulder. "You know what you need to do? Let your hair down. Live on the edge. Do something wild and spontaneous for once," she admonished.

"Ever since you started dating Tavares you've been obsessed with hooking me up," Niveah complained, running a hand through her naturally curly hair. She'd accomplished a lot in her thirty-four years, and contrary to what her girlfriends thought, she loved her life just the way it was. So what if she didn't have a husband, kids and a three-story house in the suburbs? She was successful and financially stable and that's all that mattered. "Quit badgering me, Jeanette. And for your information, I do tons of exciting things."

Roxi raised her eyebrows. "Really? Like what?"

"She's bluffing," Jeanette accused. "Niveah will do anything to stay in her boring little world, including lying about having an active social life."

"I have a lot of fun. Just last week I went rock climbing with some of the teens I mentor."

Roxi guffawed. "If that's what you call exciting, then you're worse off than I thought!"

"Niveah, you're never going to find true love if you keep hiding behind your attaché case," Jeanette told her. "You need to take a page out of my book because once I quit stressing about work and started doing activities I enjoyed, I couldn't keep the men off me. And now I have Tavares, and my life is complete."

Roxi gave Jeanette a high five. "Me, too, girlfriend. It's just a matter of time before Cedrick pops the question, and once he does, I'll be all over the Saks Fifth Avenue bridal registry!"

"If you two are so blissfully in love," Niveah challenged, "then why are you at this party?"

"Keeping your rusty butt company!"

Jeanette and Roxi roared with laughter.

"Before the night's over, I'm going to find you someone to dance with. Someone like…" Jeanette's gaze panned the crowd and after several seconds, she squealed. Bouncing up and down on her seat like an unruly toddler high on sugar, she clapped her hands and nodded her head. "Check out the hottie at the end of the bar. He's a perfect ten!"

Niveah didn't bother looking up from her drink. Jeanette's idea of good-looking was a lanky gangbanger plastered in tattoos; but Niveah preferred studious, conservative types. Not a square, just someone with manners and class, who'd treat her with respect. But as her ex-fiancé had so aptly proven nine months ago, looks were deceiving.

"That man is *beyond* fine! I'd do him in a New York minute!"

Niveah's ears perked up. If Roxi thought the stranger was fine, then he was. Despite being divorced twice, she was in the market for husband number three, and could spot a good-looking guy a block away.

Straightening in her seat, Niveah peered around the cluster of model-esque clones obscuring her view of the bar. Jeanette yanked her to the left, pointed an acrylic fingernail directly ahead, and yelled, "He's the one in the dark designer suit."

Niveah's mouth fell open.

"I told you he was perfect."

And he was. Words couldn't describe how truly gorgeous the stranger was. Bald, buff brothers didn't usually catch Niveah's eye, but this man had it seriously going on. Immaculately groomed, with clear skin, and defined features, he had a one of a kind look that instantly made her wet. His gaze was hungry, almost predatory, and his sexy mouth was rimmed with a neat, trim goatee. The brother owned the room, and the hearts of all the females in attendance—including hers. Her body hummed, and suddenly the grand ballroom felt hotter than a furnace. An aura of mystery surrounded the stranger, making him even more appealing. Staring at him, so intently, was bound to make Niveah go cross-eyed, but she didn't have the strength to look away. She was drawn to him, overtaken by a blinding sexual hunger she'd never known.

"If I had a man like that at home, I'd never leave," Roxi quipped, fanning her rosy cheeks. "I think I'll just go over and say hello."

Niveah cut her eyes at Roxi. "What about Cedrick?"

"What about him? Until he puts a ring on it, I'm keeping my options wide open."

Jeanette gripped her girlfriend's forearm, preventing her from rising from her seat. "Sit your big butt down. I picked him out for Niveah, not you."

"Girl, please. Miss Thang can't handle all that man. He's six feet tall and over two hundred pounds. He'd probably snap her skinny body in two." Cackling like a witch on a broom, she adjusted the neckline of her outfit. Roxi used every opportunity to show off her boobs, and her zipper-front dress served up an eyeful. "I on the other hand, specialize in turning out jocks, and that cutie's exactly my type."

Angry about being dissed, Niveah shot her soon-to-be *ex*-friend a scathing look. "You think you know everything about me, Roxi, but you don't. I'm every bit as daring as you are. If not more." To prove it, she stopped a passing waiter, ordered a cognac, and instructed him to deliver it to the gentleman at the end of the bar.

"Very well, ma'am. Would you care to include a message?"

Niveah shielded her mouth with the back of her hand. She

spoke only loud enough for the waiter to hear, and when he departed, she couldn't help but smile to herself.

"So you sent him a drink. Big friggin' deal. You're as straitlaced as they come, and—"

"Wanna bet?"

Roxi smirked. "I'd love to."

"Knock it off, you two," Jeanette ordered. "You sound like a couple of kids having a pissing contest on the schoolyard."

Roxi ignored her and addressed Niveah. "If I'm right about you being a Goody Two-Shoes, you'll have to hand over your new Gucci handbag. You know, the one I watched you drop a thousand dollars on at the mall yesterday."

"Okay, and I want your Oprah tickets."

Her face crumpled like a piece of paper. "B-b-but they're the tickets to her final show."

"Those are the terms. Deal or no deal?"

"You're on. That purse is going to look great with the dress I plan to wear to the show." Flashing a superior grin, she leaned forward in her chair, and rested her elbows on the table. "Did I tell you guys that Oprah will be interviewing her all-time favorite guests on the finale?"

"Only a million times," Jeanette grumbled.

"There are also rumors circulating that world-famous singers will be performing together. I can hardly wait! It's going to be…"

Having heard this before, Niveah glanced absently around the ballroom. It was no surprise that her eyes strayed to the bar. Her mouth dried. *He* was staring right at her. Guests blew noisemakers, and boisterous laughter filled the room, but Niveah could still hear her deafening heartbeat. It was beating in double-time, throbbing painfully in her ears.

Wearing a broad, megawatt smile, the handsome stranger lifted his tumbler in the air, tilted his head toward her and downed his glass in one smooth swig.

"Go over there and introduce yourself," Jeanette encouraged, brimming with excitement. "He's *definitely* interested in you, girl."

Roxi shook her head. "Miss Thang is too much of a lady to approach a guy. Attending a high siddity university made her all proper and whatnot. See, I believe in taking life by the horns, so if you'll excuse me, that hottie at the bar is calling my name."

"Then, you need to get a hearing aid, because he's checking out Niveah, not you!" Jeanette laughed at her own joke. "I know it's hard for you to believe, Roxi, but you can't have every man you want."

"Oh yes I can," she snapped, twirling her index finger around in the air, "and besides, Niveah wouldn't know the first thing to do with a brother like that."

Niveah gripped the stem of her cocktail glass to keep from shoving Roxi off her chair. They'd had a love-hate relationship ever since Jeanette introduced them, and it was at times like this that Niveah wondered why they were even friends. "We'll see about that."

Niveah downed the rest of her mai tai, pushed back her chair and stood. Her legs wobbled as she walked across the sleek hardwood floor. *I can do this. I'm smart and sexy and I have a lot to offer.* Repeating the words she'd once heard on an afterschool special didn't bolster her confidence. Niveah wished she had another drink, because as she approached the bar, she felt an intense bout of the nerves.

The stranger stood against the counter, holding his Blackberry, oblivious to her approach. As Niveah came up beside him, she tried to think of something clever to say. Anything besides the standard greeting. "I hope you're enjoying your cognac," she said, in her sultriest voice, "you strike me as the kind of man who likes a strong drink."

Damien Hunter glanced up from his cell phone and his eyes bulged out of his head like a cartoon character. Standing before him in a slinky champagne-colored dress was a caramel-skinned goddess. A woman he felt an instant, undeniable connection to.

Examining her gave Damien great pleasure, so he did a slow, thorough appraisal. He took in every detail of her face, committing each exquisite feature to memory. Her blinding white teeth drew his attention to the delicate curve of her lips. To the pretty, full rosebuds he could already feel around his—

Damien purged his thoughts. He was putting the cart before the horse. Conversation first, mind-blowing sex after.

Resting his arms against the counter, he continued his assessment. Loose, luscious curls grazed her shoulders, brushing lightly against her arms. Her mouth looked sweet, her hips were fine and he was itching to stroke her long caramel brown legs. She looked wholesome, like the kind of woman who baked bread and enjoyed playing with children, but there was nothing innocent about her sultry smile. It was provocative, tinged with lust and full of suggestion. In his profession, he mixed with a lot of attractive women, but no one had ever captured his attention like this sister with the bedroom eyes. *Play it cool, man,* the voice inside his head cautioned. *She's just another crazy beautiful woman looking for a good time, and you're just the man to give it to her.* "What's your name, beautiful?"

Niveah licked her lips. The sound of his voice, all deep and masculine, was enough to melt her panties right off. He oozed with confidence, pulsed with positive energy and smelled like expensive aftershave. "I'm Niveah. And you are?"

"Damien," he said smoothly. "I appreciate you buying me a drink, but now it's my turn to return the favor. What would you like?"

You, naked in my bed. The thought made a wave of giddiness sweep over her. *Where had that come from?* she wondered. Niveah hadn't had sex in—hell, it had been so long she couldn't remember. That's why being in close proximity of this tall, dark and handsome man made her wet in all the right places. "Two cocktails are my limit, so I'll just have a ginger ale."

While he placed the order, Niveah checked out his profile. Jeanette was right about him being good-looking, but he was much, *much* more. On top of having a smooth-as-chocolate-pudding complexion, he had a straight nose, chiseled jaw and a chest that she was aching to lick, and stroke and caress. "Thank you," she said, taking the glass he offered. Electricity passed between them when their fingers touched, and it took a moment for Niveah to recover. "Tell me about yourself, Damien."

"I'm in town on business. What about you?"

Keeping up her end of the conversation was more difficult than riding a bicycle backward. Damien was a great conversationalist, who made her laugh, asked tons of questions and listened intently to her responses, but Niveah couldn't concentrate. Her mind was all over the place, jumping from one illicit sexual thought to the next. It didn't take her long to come to a decision: she was going to sleep with Damien, and when she heard the opening bar to her favorite R & B song, Niveah imagined herself kissing him all over.

"Care to dance?"

Niveah cast a glance at the overcrowded dance floor. "Yeah, but I don't feel like getting trampled on."

"Then we'll dance right here."

Singing the lyrics to the song, Niveah moved her shoulders and legs in time with the slow, erotic beat. R. Kelly was singing about being ready and so was she. Niveah liked the way he moved, loved how cool and self-assured he was.

Caught up in the moment, she abandoned herself to the music and allowed herself to be swept into his arms. It didn't matter that they'd just met or that her girlfriends were watching; this felt right, fated, like the most natural thing in the world.

Needing to be closer to him, she curled her arms around his neck, swallowing the space that had been living between them. Niveah had never considered having a one-night stand before, but then again, she'd never met a man who looked fresh off the pages of a Ralph Lauren ad and whose voice tickled the area between her legs.

Damien drew her close. Close enough to feel her breasts. She felt soft, as delicate as a flower. Savoring the feel of her warmth, he inhaled her sweet flowery perfume. Slow dancing was the ultimate form of foreplay, and the more their bodies rubbed together, the more he wanted her. His confidence had taken a hit when his ex-girlfriend dumped him, but being approached by a woman who could win *America's Next Top Model* was a huge ego boost. Niveah wasn't shy about showing him what she liked, wasn't afraid to take the lead. Holding his gaze, she covered his hands with her own, and dragged them down her hips and across her butt.

A hard-on grew in Damien's pants. He was drowning, flailing, sinking faster than a fool in the ocean without a life jacket. One dance and he was a goner. Lost. Unable to keep a lid on his passion. What would happen when they kissed? Because it wasn't a matter of *if* it would happen, but *when* it would happen.

Desperate to taste her, he pressed his mouth against the curve of her neck. Encouraged by her deep moans, he greedily ran his hands up and down her back. Damien's head snapped up as if it had a mind of its own. *What am I doing?* He wanted this woman in his bed—tonight—but groping her in front of a room full of strangers wasn't the way to go. "I'm thirsty, you?"

"Parched," she whispered, her eyes moving slowly over his lips. "I don't live too far from here. Care to come back to my place for a nightcap?"

Damien held up a white key card. "I have a better idea. Why don't you come up to my room? Like I mentioned earlier, I'm in town on business and if you have no other plans, I'd love some company." He added, "I don't know anyone here, and hanging out with you would be a great way to kick off the year."

To buy herself some time to consider his offer, Niveah took a deep breath and slowly exhaled. Going upstairs with him was insane. Something she'd always promised herself she'd never do. At least at her house she could control the situation, but there was no telling what would happen once they were alone in his domain. But did she really want a perfect stranger—even a gorgeous one—in her personal space? Her doubts mingled with the butterflies pelting her stomach. Did it matter where they went? Niveah wanted to spend the night with Damien, wanted to experience the thrill of having a one-night stand, and as long as her friends knew where she was going to be, there was nothing to fear. "I'm going to go say goodbye to my girlfriends," she told him. "I'll meet you in the lobby in five minutes."

He nodded, squeezed her arm, then turned and walked away. Niveah watched him, admiring his long, even strides and how fine he looked in his tailored suit. Desire surged through her. She was ending the year off on a bang, and as she crossed the room toward her table, she could see the stunned expressions on her girlfriends' faces. Smiling like a beauty pageant winner, she lifted her chin and added more bounce to her step. For the first time ever, she was leaving a party with the hottest man in the room. It was a heady, intoxicating feeling.

"Welcome back, Dirty Diana!" Roxi joked.

Jeanette pointed at Niveah's empty cocktail glass. "Blame it on the alcohol is right! Exactly how many mai tais did you have?"

"I'm not drunk. That's not what this is about. We…we really connected."

"I know, we saw. Saw his hands connect with your *breast*, your ass and—"

Niveah cut Roxi off. "I'm going up to Damien's room," she explained, collecting her things. "I just wanted you guys to know where I was going so you wouldn't be worried."

"Slow down, Miss Thang. Before you rush off, let me lay down the ground rules for you."

"What ground rules?"

"For having a one-night stand," Roxi explained, sticking out her right thumb. "Don't share any personal information, use protection and the most important rule of all…"

Niveah was surprised to find herself hanging on to Roxi's every word. "Okay, okay, I got it. If it's not too late, I'll give you guys a ring when I get home."

"I don't care what time you get in. Call me. I want to hear all the scandalous details!"

Niveah hugged her girlfriends, grabbed her purse and marched off.

"She'll have second thoughts before she reaches the elevator."

"You don't think she'll go through with it?" Jeanette asked, watching their friend depart.

Roxi snickered. "There's no way in hell!"

Chapter 2

Damien studied his gold Concord watch. He'd been waiting in the lobby for fifteen minutes, but there was still no sign of Niveah. Where was she? Had she changed her mind? The curvy, fresh-faced beauty could have any man she wanted in the grand ballroom, and there was a very good chance she'd hooked up with someone else.

He raked a hand over his head, trying to decide what to do next. In an effort to regroup, Damien breathed in deeply through his nose. He considered returning to the party to scope out another playmate lookalike, but decided against it. The truth was, he didn't want anyone else. He wanted the sister with the curly hair, caramel complexion, and smokin' hot body.

To block out the images of Niveah flashing in his mind, Damien shut his eyes. It didn't help. He saw them kissing, fondling, tearing at each other's clothes. Just as he was about to hit the climax of his X-rated dream, he heard someone call his name. Damien turned in time to see Niveah sail through the ballroom doors.

Desire zipped up his spine.

Hotter than the lead girl in a rap music video, she stared right at him, oblivious to the googly-eyed expressions on the faces of the other men in the lobby. Damien had always been a sucker for a big butt and a smile, and the sister sauntering toward him had both. Her high heels gave her legs incredible definition, and he imagined himself running his hands up her smooth, toned calves. Sexy wasn't how a woman looked or what she wore, it was her attitude; and he could tell by the way Niveah moved that she was in a sexy state of mind. Perfect. Maybe they could skip the useless chitchat, and get right down to business.

"Sorry to keep you waiting."

On the outside, Damien was as calm as the Rock of Gibraltar, but when Niveah placed a hand on his forearm, he felt himself unraveling. It took everything he had not to crush his mouth against her pretty pink lips. "It's no sweat. I used the time to check the messages on my cell."

Niveah gestured to the grand ballroom. "They're doing the electric slide in there and it was crazy getting through the crowd. I thought I was going to get swept away."

"No worries, beautiful. You're definitely worth the wait."

Her smile widened. "You certainly have a way with words."

"I've heard that a time or two before."

"I bet you have."

They shared a laugh.

Damien jabbed the elevator button and almost cheered when the doors immediately slid open. The sooner they got to his room, the sooner he could see her naked. Allowing her to go first, he examined her pear-shaped figure with wide eyes and a dry mouth. The clingy dress material swished over her hips, outlining her round, juicy butt. Damien hoped she was wearing a thong. That was his favorite piece of lingerie and just thinking about squeezing, and smacking her ass made his pulse hammer in his chest. "Are you hungry?' he asked, wanting to fill the awkward silence. "I could order something up from room service if you'd like."

"I've never done this sort of thing before." The words seemed to burst out of her mouth, and for the first time since meeting her she seemed shy, scared. "I've dated some over the years, but I've never had…a one-night stand."

Amused, he pressed the button for the twentieth floor. If he had a dime for every time a woman had fed him that line he could buy the car of his dreams—a black Rolls Royce Phantom.

"I don't want to give you the wrong impression of me. I'm not the kind of girl who…"

Why did women always do this? he wondered, concealing a grin. *Did they think pretending they were actually* good girls gone bad for the night *would improve his opinion of them?* The muscles in his jaw tightened. *Right, like* that *was ever going to happen.* If there was one thing he'd learned through traveling the globe, it was that women enjoyed sex. As much, if not more, than men did. And those with sexual hang-ups had been programmed by their parents and well-meaning Sunday school teachers into believing only whores liked doing the nasty. But Damien was here to tell Niveah that it was okay to embrace her sexuality. She was a freak, a woman who loved casual sex, and there was nothing wrong with that. "Tonight's about being in the moment, about being free without restrictions."

"I think I made a mistake." Niveah rubbed a hand along her forehead, then dragged it through her hair. "My friends were ganging up on me, and I let what they said get to me. I approached you at the bar to prove to them that I can be fun and spontaneous, but the truth is I'm not. I'm really sorry about all this, but I have to go back downstairs to the…"

Damien blinked, sure the cognac he'd downed earlier was blurring his vision. The sexy, flirtatious woman he'd met at the bar less than an hour ago was crumbling right before his eyes. And if he didn't do something quick, their night of passionate lovemaking would be ruined. Realizing their evening was in jeopardy, Damien sprang to action. He stepped forward, pulled her to his chest and planted one on her. A kiss so fierce their bodies slammed together.

Niveah fought against him, trying to escape, but gave up the fight when he inclined his head toward her, deepening the kiss. Bolts of electricity shot between them. He'd initiated contact, but feeling her lips against his sent Damien stumbling back into the mirrored wall. Had he ever tasted a mouth so soft? So wickedly sweet and enticing?

Unsteady on his feet, he clutched her waist. They grunted and groaned, caressed and squeezed until it became unbearable. Damien stuck a hand up her dress, and cursed fashion designers for ever inventing such a tight, restrictive material. A little piece of fabric wasn't going to prevent him from copping a feel, he decided, using his hands to yank down the sheer barrier.

Palming her butt cheeks, he ground his erection into her, loving how soft she felt against his body. Damien slid a hand inside her panties, and Niveah purred in his ear. He played in her hair, twirling curls around his index finger. Then he probed her core with his thumb. A thick, creamy moisture oozed onto his hand. Her clit was wet, slick—just the way he liked it. He hadn't tasted her yet, hadn't dipped his mouth inside the treasure between her legs, but he could already feel the righteous makings of a killer orgasm. "I can't wait to be inside you," he whispered. "That's what you want, isn't it? For me to sex you all night long?"

Her tortured moans filled the air.

Damien withdrew his hand from in between Niveah's legs and frantically searched his pockets. They weren't going to make it to his suite. Not when she was bucking against him like a wild woman on a runaway bull. He retrieved the condom just as the elevator doors slid open.

Niveah surfaced from her haze. It was a miracle she was still standing. Voices carried down the hall, reminding her that she was still at the Ritz-Carlton, and not back in her bedroom playing out a hot, torrid fantasy. Since she didn't want to kick off the year flashing perfect strangers in a hotel she frequented for business, she straightened her dress, and yanked up her stockings. *How the hell did my stilettos come off?* she wondered, stuffing her feet back into her red Fendi shoes. *Probably somewhere between Damien palming my breasts, and fingering my clit,* she surmised, still feeling the after affects of her mini-orgasm.

Niveah almost lost her balance when Damien seized her hand. "This way," he said, making a sharp left turn. "My suite is at the end of the hall."

A green light flashed when Damien slid his key card into the slot above the door. Opening it with one hand, he gently urged her inside with the other. Niveah almost stumbled over her feet. This was actually going to happen; she was about to have her first one-night stand. Doubts attacked her like invisible assailants hiding in the dark. Her mind was screaming, *No, don't do it!,* but her body was screaming, *Yes! Yes! Yes!* What the hell was she supposed to do?

Warmed by Damien's good-natured smile, she shoved her fears aside and stepped farther into the suite. The air smelled like men's aftershave, and the light from the moon spilling in through the balcony created a peaceful, tranquil mood.

Damien came up behind her, so close that she could feel his erection through her dress. Goose bumps broke out across her arm. He—Niveah gulped—couldn't be that long, could he? He gripped her shoulders, then buried his face into her hair. Damien placed kisses along the slope of her neck, and her head fell flat against his chest. Using his hands, he tweaked her nipples and massaged her clit simultaneously.

A fire brewed in Niveah's stomach, causing her to moan. The ache between her legs grew to a full-blown throb. Then her heart got into the mix, skipping, thumping, rattling. Niveah never knew it could be like this. Never knew that she could want someone this much.

It started with a surge in her chest, then uncontrollable shaking and shortness of breath. Before she could ward against the onslaught, several fast, hard climaxes gripped her. Pleasure exploded behind Niveah's eyes. Damien was going to kill her. Right here in the middle of his luxurious executive suite. Her desire for him couldn't be contained, and she was quickly losing control. Screaming, grunting, begging Damien for more.

Time slipped away. Stretched into passion-filled seconds and minutes.

Niveah didn't know how much more of this she could take. It was just a matter of time before she was gasping for air and her legs gave way. Moaning in sweet agony, she arched her back, fully prepared to ride out another looming orgasm. Damien cupped her chin, and kissed her so fully, so passionately, Niveah felt as if she was spinning on a carousel. Her shoes fell off, her dress sailed down her hips, and her fifty-dollar nylons lay in pieces on the floor.

Still kissing, they stumbled farther into the suite, knocking into end tables, couch legs and other furniture. Down to just her panties, her body throbbing with heat and desire, she dragged her fingernails up his chest, across his neck, and over his head. Moving to an inaudible beat, Niveah rocked her hips against his shaft. Grinding her backside into his crotch caused Damien to release a savage groan. Wanting to give as much as she'd received, Niveah reached around, unzipped his pants and massaged his erection. Touching him confirmed it. The brother was hung. Like Mandingo. Long, thick and righteously built.

Damien swiveled his tongue around her nipples, licked between her breasts and trailed his mouth down her spine. Niveah sucked in a breath, sure she was about to black out. The more aggressive Damien was, the more turned-on she was. Everything about him was erotically charged and exciting. He had great hands, hands a masseur would kill for, and he knew how she liked to be touched. Damien kissed like he was making love to her mouth, thrilled her every time he nuzzled his face against the curve of her ear, and whispered dirty commands in that deep, throaty tone. His voice, like his smile and gaze, made her weak.

Is this for real, or am I dreaming? Niveah wondered, feeling light-headed and free.

Undressing faster than a superhero in a telephone booth, Damien ripped open a gold packet, protected himself with the Magnum condom, and bent Niveah over the closest chair. "Spread your legs. Spread them nice and wide for me."

Niveah did as she was told, and was rewarded with a kiss on her shoulder. Damien pulled her hair, great big handfuls, as he positioned himself between her legs. He piqued her pleasure when he caressed her butt, tenderly, lovingly. His stroke felt great on her neck, back and thighs.

"You feel like heaven," he praised, gliding his hands up her hips to her breasts. This woman—not the Mona Lisa—was the finest work of art he'd ever seen, but when Damien told Niveah she was gorgeous, she laughed. "You don't believe me?" Damien cupped her chin. The heat of his gaze torched her flesh, made her feel as if she was on display. "Since you don't believe me, I guess I'll have to show you."

Slowly, he slid his penis along her clit. Back and forth until she cried out. Begged. Pleaded. Cursed. Demanded he slip inside her. When he finally did, she released a torrent of screams. Niveah pressed her face into a cushion to muffle her moans. This wasn't like her. Only porn stars groaned and grunted during sex. That's what they were paid for. To play it up for the cameras. But the more Damien swiveled his lips, the louder, more intense her groans became.

Feet firmly planted on the ground, she held on to the arms of the padded chair and rocked her hips against his groin. Damien swelled inside her. At least three inches. He hit all of her hot spots, and created body-quivering sensations that brought tears to her eyes. With his hands and his words, he took her to new heights and deeper depths.

Her breathing picked up.

Her moans intensified.

The room spun faster, and faster.

Colors—vivid pinks and whites and red—exploded behind Niveah's eyes, causing her to choke back a deep, racking sob.

"Damn!" Damien pulled out, then turned her to face him. "Are you okay? Did I hurt you?"

Niveah shook her head. "You didn't hurt me. I just…" Embarrassed, she lowered her eyes to the floor. "It just felt so good that…that it made me a little emotional. That's all."

"We'll stop. The last thing I wanted to do was cause you pain or make tonight all about me. I lost control and I feel like an ass for…"

Niveah wanted to scream. *Why wasn't he listening to her? Couldn't he tell how incredible he was making her feel?* To end his rant, she placed a finger against his lips, cutting him off. "This night is far from over. I plan to finish what *you* started, even if it takes all night."

Full of energy and determination, she circled his nipple with her tongue, licking, teasing, stroking. She wanted to ravage him, prove to herself that she was a good lover, that the accusations her ex-fiancé had leveled at her the night of their breakup were unfounded. To show him that she was in charge, that the tables had turned and that she was running the show, Niveah grabbed his butt and gave it an extra hard squeeze. Her breathing was shallow, and her body was burning up, but Niveah wanted more. A lot more kissing, teasing and licking.

"Are you sure about this, Niveah?" Concern touched his features, and his eyes were crinkled at the corners. "I don't want you to have any regrets. Not one."

Niveah lifted his hand, seized his index finger and eased it inside her. She felt naughty, dangerous and in complete control. It was a feeling she could easily get high off. A deep sigh fell from between Niveah's lips as Damien's fingers probed her core, and when she finally spoke her voice was several octaves lower. "You feel how wet I am? You did this to me, Damien, and the only regret I have is not approaching you sooner."

"I didn't know you were such a bad girl."

"You haven't seen nothin' yet."

Easily, he lifted her up off the floor. Grabbing a fistful of her hair, he swooped down, and feasted on her lips. Niveah folded her arms around his neck, and wrapped her legs around his slim, muscular torso. Feeling sexier than a Maxim swimsuit model, she nipped at his earlobe, then eagerly sucked it into her mouth.

On the king-size bed they laughed and played, lost in their exhilarating private world. They were in perfect sync, moving naturally together, as graceful as a pair of ballroom dancers. An hour in, and countless orgasms later, Niveah was begging Damien to climax. "I don't know how much more of this I can take!"

"I'm nowhere near being ready," he announced, thrusting his hips, plunging deeper still. "You feel so damn good, I may never come…"

"We'll see about that." Niveah flicked her tongue against his ear, and he cooed. Propping up her elbows, she loosened her legs from around his waist, and rotated her hips in tight, fast circles.

Damien swore.

To achieve the intended outcome, Niveah added her mouth to the equation. Placing kisses on his neck, his erect, chocolate-brown nipples and all over his chest. Realizing she'd weakened her prey, she went in for the kill. In one swift movement, Niveah had Damien flat on his back. His eyes widened in surprise, causing Niveah to giggle. Keeping her head up, her back straight, she lowered herself onto his lap and released a deep, satisfying groan.

Squeezing her pelvic muscles held Damien firmly in place, and before she could put any of those childhood horseback riding lessons to good use, he gripped her hips, gave a powerful, thrust and collapsed onto the mound of pillows beneath him. "Damn, baby, *that* was incredible."

Niveah licked the dryness from her lips. "I couldn't agree more."

"If I knew you were such an animal in bed, I would have updated my will!" he teased, pulling her to his chest.

Niveah tensed. Her friends said cuddling was against the rules, so she was surprised when Damien spread the blanket over them and wrapped his arms around her. *Shouldn't I be dressed and on my way out the door? Isn't this how these things usually worked?*

Sweat clung to her skin, and matted clumps of hair were stuck to her shoulders, but Damien was smiling at her as if she was the most beautiful thing he had ever seen. His grip was fierce, protective, unlike anything she'd ever experienced. The hotel suite smelled like sex, and a hot stifling air that made Niveah feel as if she was trapped inside an oven.

"I don't want to get up, but if I don't get something to drink I'm going to die of dehydration," he joked, swinging his feet over the side of the bed. "What can I get you?"

"I'll have what you're having." Swathing the bed sheet

across her chest, she carefully tucked it under her arms, and braced her body against the headboard. "Better yet, make mine a double!"

Damien chuckled as he switched on the bedside lamp. "We should order up some room service. I'm starving, and I bet you are, too."

As if on cue, her stomach growled. "I can't. I have to get going."

"Why, do you have someone waiting for you at home?" Damien picked up the phone, but his gaze remained locked on her face. "Things happened so fast, I forgot to ask if you had a man."

"If I did, I wouldn't be here with you," she told him, unsure of what to make of his comment.

"Then stay and have dinner with me."

Niveah opened her mouth to decline, but when he smiled at her, she caved. "If you're sure you don't mind me staying a little while longer, I'd love a bite to eat. I'm not picky when it comes to food, anything will be fine."

"I'd like to order an extra-large deep-dish pizza with everything on it, and the twenty-piece buffalo wings," he said, into the phone. "Bill it to my suite, and ask the concierge to leave the cart outside the door. I don't want to be disturbed."

Damien ended the call, took two sodas out of the fridge and handed one to her. "Why don't you tell me more about yourself? I'm curious to why a woman like you is still on the market."

"Funny, I was just wondering the same thing about you."

"Are you trying to dodge the question?" He wore a serious expression, but Niveah could see the makings of a smile on his lips. "Are you between lovers or playing the field like me?"

"None of the above. I'm married to my work, and I don't have time to date. I was engaged last year, but it didn't work out. We…we wanted different things." Niveah glanced out the window. It had been a year since Stewart left her for another woman—someone younger, and more adventurous in bed—but every time she thought about their breakup, she felt a pang in her chest. He wasn't ever coming back so why was she thinking about him? "What do you think of Tampa? It's nothing like the Big Apple, but I bet you're loving the weather."

"What makes you think I'm from the East Coast?"

Niveah laughed. "No offense, but you could be the poster child for NYC. The cocky, bad-boy swagger instantly gave you away, and if that's not enough, you have an accent, too."

"All right, you got me," he admitted, drowning the rest of his soda and grabbing another one. "I grew up in the Bronx. And you're right about the weather. Every time I come down here for business, I think about relocating permanently!"

They laughed.

"I'll be right back." Damien got up off the bed, and strode out of the bedroom. Niveah watched him leave, marveling at his utterly perfect body. Resisting the urge to scream into her pillow, she smoothed a hand over her cheeks and ran a hand through her wild, unruly hair, knowing she could give the winner of the Atlanta Hair Show a run for their money.

Spotting the remote, she picked it up from off the nightstand, and pointed it at the black entertainment unit. *Why am I still sitting here watching TV? This is the perfect opportunity for me to break free.* Niveah tried to get off the bed, but her limbs were asleep.

Hearing a door slam, she strained her eyes toward the foyer. The scent of mozzarella cheese hit her nose and Niveah licked her lips. Twice. All thoughts of leaving evaporated into thin air when Damien walked into the bedroom and placed the box of pizza on the nightstand.

"Dig in, beautiful. You've worked up quite an appetite tonight."

Niveah dove right in, helping herself to a large, gooey slice, but she couldn't help thinking the whole scene was a little strange. She was sitting in bed eating pizza and buffalo wings with her one-night stand.

"Cool, Robin Thicke is about to perform. That dude's got amazing chops!"

"I'm impressed. Most men would never admit to being a fan."

"I never said I thought the guy was cute. I said he could sing. Nothing wrong with that."

Niveah bit into her pizza. It was hot and loaded—just the way she liked it, and if Damien didn't hurry up and start eating, there'd be none left. "Everyone has their weakness, and mine is definitely junk food," she said, chewing slowly. "Oh, and coffee. I drink five, sometimes six cups a day. It all depends on how bad things are going at the office."

"You must have a very demanding career."

"It's not my job that's going to kill me, it's my lazy, dimwitted employees!" Shaking her head, she wiped the oil off her hands with a napkin. "If they did everything they were assigned to do, I wouldn't be so stressed out, but I'm always having to correct their mistakes and it's exhausting. I swear, one of these days I'm going to replace every last one of them!"

Damien chuckled. "It sounds like you need a little TLC."

"You have no idea."

His hands traveled up her thigh, and Niveah purred in anticipation, knowing exactly where they were going next. *Higher, higher, higher dammit!*

"Why don't you let me show you what you've been missing?" he whispered, pulling her down on top of him and running his hands over her butt. "By the time I'm done tapping this ass, you won't have a care in the world."

Chapter 3

"Here's the rundown of your morning," Doris Murphy began, opening her black portfolio notebook. "You have a staff meeting at nine o'clock, coffee with the marketing department an hour later and lunch with Vladimir Butkovsky at noon."

Niveah consulted her agenda. "I'm expecting to hear from Mrs. Garrett-Reed today. If she calls while I'm in the morning meeting, come and get me. Understand?"

"Yes, Ms. Evans. Is there anything else? If not, I'll return to my desk and finish typing up your notes from last night's brainstorming session."

Spotting a male figure striding by her office, Niveah leaned sideways in her chair, and peered around her receptionist's full-figured frame. "Have you seen the new guy?"

"Mr. Hunter just arrived with Mr. Russo. Apparently, the two had breakfast this morning."

Niveah didn't like the sound of that. It was bad enough her boss had hand-picked this clown to work on *her* project, but discovering they were socializing off the clock was upsetting.

She'd have to keep a close eye on this Hunter character. Her first crack at him would be at the morning staff meeting, and Niveah had every intention of showing him who was really in charge of the project. First she'd make him her new best friend, and then she'd pull the rug out from underneath him. The thought brought a smile to her lips.

"Confirm my twelve-thirty reservations at Casa Barcelona, and give me a buzz when the rest of the team files into the conference room."

Niveah waited until her executive assistant closed the door before signing into her computer and reading the day's emails. Knowing she would be interrupted in the next ten minutes, she decided against working on her latest project. Instead, she picked up the file marked "Specifics" that Doris had brought her, and began reading.

Crossing her legs, she settled into her seat and read the document cover sheet. Excitement surged through her. This was the project she'd been waiting for her whole career. A multi-million-dollar campaign that would garner enormous press. Landing this account would not only impress the higher-ups at head office, it would improve her chances of being named vice president when Mr. Whitmore retired in the fall. The position meant long, insane hours, but also a huge pay increase. Enough money to buy her parents a lavish new home in a gated community.

Niveah thought about what she had to do. Her job was simple. Create a unique ad campaign for Discreet Boutiques and knock her colleagues out of the running for the top position. If she nailed next month's presentation, she'd be one step closer to landing her dream job. Becoming creative director six years ago had been a major accomplishment, but being named as the company's first female vice president would make headlines around the world. And Niveah wasn't above outwitting the competition to make it happen, either. That's why she was going to march into the conference room at nine o'clock sharp, and charm the socks off the clown from head office.

Niveah had perused the file a few days earlier, but she wanted to ensure she hadn't overlooked anything. Mrs. Garrett-Reed was a force to be reckoned with, and when she met the self-made woman last month, they hit it off immediately. With sales in the millions, Discreet Boutique was one of the most lucrative companies in the world, and launching a menswear line next winter was sure to triple profits.

As Niveah read from her notes, she recalled her hour-long conversation with Mrs. Garrett-Reed the previous week. Not only was she impressed by the keenness of the businesswoman's mind, but she'd been blown away by her knowledge of marketing and advertising.

"Our new menswear line was created with today's businessman in mind. Someone athletic, charismatic and successful who can finagle millions from clients, play golf with more finesse than a PGA champion and make women of all ages go gaga."

A picture of Damien sprawled flat on his back flashed in Niveah's head. It had been seventy-two hours since her one-night stand, and she'd thought of nothing else since. Niveah had a staff meeting to prep for, but she couldn't seem to get the brown-eyed New Yorker with the killer swag out of her mind. Sex with Damien had been hot, erotic and everything she'd been looking for. *Was he still staying at the Ritz-Carlton? Or had he returned home already?*

Shaking off the thought, she returned her attention to the file. It didn't matter. They'd had their fun and that was that. *So why couldn't she stop thinking about him? Why was she replaying every moment of their night together?* Niveah hated to admit it, but he'd loved her in a way no one else had before. Not even Stewart—and they'd dated for three years.

Allowing her mind to wander, she recalled how they'd made love again after eating dinner in bed. Unlike the first time they'd made love, he'd tenderly and gently stroked her. Cupping her face in his hands, sprinkling kisses on her cheeks, whispering words of praise in her ear. He'd loved her up all night long, and she still had the sore muscles to prove it.

Niveah shook her head. It was still hard to believe that she'd had sex with a perfect stranger. Part of her was angry at herself for not getting his phone number. She would have loved hooking up again, loved spending a second or even third night with him. But deep down she knew that would have been a huge mistake. Now was not the time to indulge in a seedy affair. She had a job to do, and it was imperative that she stay focused. Besides, Damien was hardly the relationship type. He was the kind of guy who promised to call at the end of a great date but didn't, who dated three women at the same time and lived for the thrill of the chase. No, she was definitely better off alone.

"The staff meeting is about to start." Her assistant's voice came through the intercom loud and clear. "Mr. Russo just walked in the conference room with the new guy, and everyone's clamoring for his attention."

Prepared to meet the enemy, she stood, buttoned her blazer and checked her appearance in the full-length mirror behind the door. Her Chanel power suit was a chic, loose-fitting design and her Gucci eyeglasses gave her a mature, intelligent air. To complete her all-business look, she'd skipped the makeup, pulled her hair back in a no-nonsense bun and passed on accessories.

In the mirror, Niveah practiced a tight, toothless smile. Perfect. She looked serious, almost deadly—like the kind of person you didn't mess with. A grin surfaced, quickly overwhelming the corners of her mouth. No one was going to push her around, especially not some hotshot from back east who Mr. Russo had hand-picked to be the next VP.

On the walk over to the conference room, Niveah went over her game plan. Befriending this Hunter guy was definitely the way to go. She'd play nice, work with him closely, then knock his feet out from under him. Guilt pricked her conscience, but she brushed all second thoughts aside. The advertising world was a ruthless, cutthroat business. To succeed at Access Media and Entertainment a girl had to play dirty, and that was exactly what Niveah intended to do.

Inside the conference room, her colleagues mingled at the breakfast table, grabbing coffees, chatting and munching on pastries and fruit. Starving, but too nervous to eat, she scoured the room for her boss. He was standing over by the window. Beside him was a much shorter man with sunken cheeks and sandy brown hair. Bingo. Mr. Hunter in the flesh. Deciding this was the perfect opportunity to introduce herself, she strode over.

"Good morning, gentlemen," Niveah greeted. "It's another gorgeous day in Tampa, isn't it?"

Damien frowned. That voice. That scent. He shook off the thought that sprang in his mind. No way. It couldn't be her. He'd been thinking about his sexy one-night stand for the last seventy-two hours, and if he didn't stop daydreaming, Mr. Russo would show him to the door. Damien refused to let that happen. After twelve years in the business, he was ready for the big leagues. Blowing this opportunity would earn him a one-way ticket back to New York, and since he had no intention of returning to the cold, corrupt city, it was time to get his head in the game.

Tearing his gaze away from the window, he turned, prepared to meet the woman who was talking amicably to his assistant.

"*This* is Damien Hunter," Mr. Russo said, clapping a hand on his shoulder. "Damien, I'd like you to meet, Niveah Evans. Like you, she's one of our brightest and most talented…"

Damien stopped breathing.

Then, his whole body turned ice-cold.

It was her.

The woman he'd had hot, passionate sex with three nights earlier. The same woman who'd swiped his platinum watch and tiptoed out of his suite while he was in the shower. Damien's mouth fell open, but nothing came out. Suddenly, he didn't know up from down, right from left, or something as rudimentary as his first and last names.

"Over the next eight weeks," his boss continued, oblivious to his physical distress, "the two of you will be heading up the Discreet Boutique menswear campaign, and I don't have to tell either one of you that there's a lot riding on this."

Ride me, baby. Faster! Faster! Faster! She'd increased her pace, rocking her hips expertly, powerfully, with more zeal than a veteran pole dancer.

Damien snapped his eyes shut, deleting the image from his mind. He ordered himself to get a grip. To return to the present and quit reliving the past. What happened with this Niveah chick was a one-time deal, and if he wanted be the next vice president of Access Media and Entertainment, he had to obliterate all thoughts of last Saturday from his mind.

The atmosphere was charged with tension, and Damien had the strange feeling that he was being watched. A glance over his shoulder confirmed it. Several women were staring at him. Had Niveah told her colleagues about the night they spent together? Did they know he'd gone down on her repeatedly? Damien stamped out the thought. Before this morning, she didn't know who he was. Or did she? Fear burned in his lungs. What if…what if their hooking up hadn't been a chance meeting? What if it had all been a setup? A scheme to blackmail him? It was a real and frightening possibility. In his twelve-year advertising career he'd seen it all. Powerful, accomplished men brought down by scandals. Even when the rumors turned out to be false, their careers were damaged irrevocably.

His features hardened and it hurt to smile. Not that he had reason to. He'd given Niveah the best sex of her life, and now she was playing him. Acting like he was a nobody. A scrub. A bugaboo. But what did he expect from a thief? Damien didn't know why he was surprised. This was the nature of women. To lie, steal and cheat. They were sharks, every last one of them. Isn't that what he'd learned from a long list of ex-girlfriends?

"I look forward to working with you, Mr. Hunter."

Without missing a beat, he nodded and extended his hand. "Likewise, Ms. Evans."

He searched her face for a sign of recognition, for acknowledgement, for something that indicated she knew who he was. Nothing. Not a blush, not a smile, not even a blink. *Isn't this a bitch,* he thought, glaring at her. *She's pulling a Bill Clinton. Pretending we didn't have sex all night long. Well, I'll show her!*

"If you're not busy this afternoon, I'd like to sit down with you and discuss the—"

Damien spoke over her. "There are a few people in the production department that I'd like to have a word with first," he lied smoothly. "Again, it was nice meeting you."

Moving on, he introduced himself to everyone in attendance, shaking hands and making note of those he'd be working with on the Discreet Boutique menswear campaign. Damien was just starting to relax when he heard Mr. Russo call his name. "Damien," he boomed, beckoning him with a large, beefy hand. "Come over here. I'd like you to say a few words."

Damien coughed. For him, public speaking was as natural as breathing, but he suddenly felt out of his element. Feeling as inept as a nine-year-old delivering the opening address at the G8 Summit, he advanced slowly toward his boss.

Underneath Damien's suit jacket, sweat soaked through his white designer dress shirt. And it didn't help that Niveah's eyes were all over him. Her gaze, filled with loathing and disgust, burned a basketball-size hole in his forehead. To remove the bitter taste in his mouth, he snatched a plastic cup off the refreshment table and downed the orange juice in one gulp.

"I know you've all had the pleasure of meeting the newest member of our team, but I'd like to formally introduce everyone to Damien Hunter. In the last decade, he's crafted some of our most memorable ads, and I'm excited to have such a creative talent on board with us."

"Thanks for the warm welcome, Mr. Russo. I'll keep this brief, because I know you're all anxious to get back to work, right?"

Polite laughter and smiles rose across the room.

"Like all of you in here, I strive to be the best in my field." To ensure he was heard above the hum of the coffee machine, he raised his voice. "Forty years ago, the founders of this great company set out with a dream. A dream to set the advertising industry on its heels with their unique ads, slogans and media spots. I'm thrilled to be working with such a creative, go-getting bunch, and I'm confident that with hard work, commitment, and collaborative input, we'll have a successful year filled with more profits and promotions."

Fervent applause followed.

Damien snuck a look at Niveah and wished he hadn't. She was inspecting her French manicure, a bored, uninterested expression on her face. He felt the urge to kick her chair, or give her shoulders a good hard shake. It was hard to believe this was the same woman who'd dropped to her knees, grabbed his package and given him the best oral sex of his life.

Niveah raised her head. There was a warning look in her eyes, and he read the message clearly: *say a word and you're a dead man*. For now he'd play her game, but this was far from over. Disgust clogged his nostrils as he watched her. Niveah Evans was one hell of an actress. Drama students should take pointers from her, he decided, sliding a hand into his pocket. Recalling how she'd screamed and cursed as she climaxed, made him grin. The creative director might be able to fool their colleagues, but he knew the real Niveah Evans. The sultry, bad-ass chick who was a freak between the sheets.

Damien examined her. Remembering how she'd purred when he'd sucked her nipples into his mouth made it impossible for him to stare at anything but her chest. He dragged his gaze back up her face, only to have it dip back down to her cleavage seconds later. Worldly wise, there wasn't much that got past him, and one glance at Niveah, sitting all prim and proper in her padded chair, told him she was a fraud. A fake. A woman with more faces than Lady Gaga. Why else would she look like a sex kitten on New Year's Eve and a sexually repressed librarian three days later? Niveah was trying to pull the wool over his eyes, but he wasn't having it. Before the end of the work day, he was going to get to the bottom of things—and retrieve his watch—because no one tricked him and got away with it.

"Dammit, Jeanette! Quit laughing, this is serious!"

"I can't help it," she admitted, still tittering, "This sounds like an episode of *Desperate Housewives,* and you know how much I love that show!"

More giggles flowed over the phone line.

Niveah leaned against the tiled wall and crossed an arm under her chest. Sneaking off to the bathroom in the middle of the staff meeting to call Jeanette was risky, but she couldn't handle being in the conference room a second longer. Not with her hands and legs shaking furiously. Shocked didn't begin to describe how she felt when her boss introduced her to Damien Hunter. Ashamed and mortified were more suitable words, but she wasn't about to tell her best friend that. Besides, Jeanette was too busy busting a gut to realize the severity of the situation. "I can't believe this is happening. This is my worst nightmare come true, and you're cracking up like you're watching a Chris Rock HBO special."

"Girl, I'm sorry, but this is just too rich!" Her tone was

filled with awe. "Okay, let me make sure I got this straight. Your one-night stand—the guy you had, and I quote, 'the most amazing sex of your life with'—is the clown from the East Coast office? The man Mr. Russo expects you to work with on that big Discreet Boutique account?"

Niveah cringed. Again.

"I could kick myself for calling in sick today. I would have given anything to see the look on your face when that Damien guy came into the conference room."

"Believe me, it wasn't pretty."

"I bet. You've gotten yourself into one hell of a jam, and I'm dying to know what you're going to do next."

"Nail the Discreet Boutique campaign, that's what."

"No, not about work, about this Damien guy. Are you going to approach him, or pretend your rumble in the jungle didn't happen?"

"Can you stop saying that?" Niveah snapped. "It's not funny."

"You were the one who said the sex was wild and primitive, like two animals mating in the jungle," she said innocently. "Now back to my original question, are you going to talk to—"

"Why would I do that? We had our fun, and now it's time to move on. I have a campaign to finish, and a presentation to prep for. I don't have time to worry about some man I…" *had hot, steamy sex with.* The words rose in her thoughts, but she said, "I've already forgotten about."

"I wouldn't be able to work with someone I've had sex with, but if anyone can do it, you can. Your employees don't call you 'the Heart of Darkness' for nothing."

The bathroom door swung open, and two women from the human resources department sauntered inside. "Hello, Ms. Evans," they greeted.

Niveah nodded, then whispered into the phone. "We'll talk later."

"Sure thing. Try not to worry. Everything will be fine."

Doubtful of that being true, she ended the call, switched off her cell phone and slid it into her jacket pocket. Determined to make a hasty getaway, Niveah reached for the door handle.

"What do you think of the new guy?"

Niveah glanced over her shoulder, realized the brunette was speaking to her, and plastered a smile on her face. Each company had at least one employee who lived for gossip, but Access Media and Entertainment had been cursed with two, and since she didn't want to be the next casualty on the rumormill, she decided to be nice to the Olsen twin lookalikes. "I only spoke to him briefly, but he seemed okay. Why?"

"The female employees are placing bets on who will nail him first. Essence Jackson, over in the finance department, is leading the pack."

What was with the women betting all of a sudden? Snippets of her conversation with Roxi on New Year's filled her mind. A cold shiver crawled up her back, and a scowl tightened the corners of her lips. Her friend was to blame for the trouble she was in. If Roxi hadn't goaded her into having a one-night stand, she wouldn't be hiding out in the women's washroom now. Okay, so Roxi hadn't had put a revolver to her head and forced her to have sex with Damien, but Niveah needed someone to blame and big-mouth Roxi was it.

"Damien Hunter puts the *f* in fine, and if I wasn't happily married, I'd be all over him."

I hear you, girlfriend, I hear you.

The shorter woman stopped preening in the mirror, a contemplative expression on her oval-shaped face. "I don't know what it is, but every time he looks at me I get knots in my stomach and I break out in goose bumps. It's the strangest thing."

Tell me something I don't know, Niveah thought, remembering the first time she'd seen Damien at the Ritz-Carlton bar. Six feet tall, dreamy eyes, shrouded with muscles.

He was confident, persuasive and smoking hot. What more could a woman want? And then there was that dark, penetrating gaze of his. The sexual energy between them was crushing, the single most devastating thing she'd ever experienced. His voice had had a calm, soporific effect on her, and before she knew what she was doing, they were headed upstairs to his executive suite. There, he'd further broken down her defenses, making her believe with every kiss that it had never been like this for him.

"A bunch of us thought it would be fun to take Damien out for drinks after work," she continued, turning back to the mirror. "If you don't have other plans, you're more than welcome to join us. We're meeting at the bar up the block around five."

Curious, Niveah asked who was going.

"Everyone," they answered in unison. "Since there'll be over twenty of us, I went ahead and made reservations for one of their back corner rooms. That way we can talk and mingle, and drink our martinis in peace."

"Thanks for the invitation, but I'm afraid I can't join you. I'm working late tonight."

"I told you she wouldn't come," grumbled the shorter woman to her friend. "She doesn't believe in fraternizing with her subordinates, remember?"

Anxious for the conversation to end, Niveah yanked open the bathroom door. She hurried out into the hall, and ran smack dab into her wickedly handsome one-night stand.

Chapter 4

"You, in my office, *now.*"

Niveah's apology died on her lips. Where the hell did Damien get off yelling at her? She was the most successful creative buyer at Access Media and Entertainment, not some flunky in the mailroom sorting envelopes. Instead of saying sorry, Niveah asked Damien if he was out of his damn mind. "Who do you think you're talking to? I'm not your subordinate, I'm your equal. And don't you ever forget it. I deserve to be treated with respect and—"

"Not here." The sharpness of his tone put an end to her rant. "Follow me."

Without as much as a nod, he strode past her. The thought of being alone with Damien petrified her, but when he turned the corner, Niveah had no choice but to follow. She watched him open the door to his left and frowned. Curious as to why he wanted them to talk in the storage room, she hurried to catch up.

As she entered, her feet slowed, and her eyes widened.

Where was she when they'd transformed the dark, dingy space into something Martha Stewart would be proud of? The room smelled like freshly squeezed lemons and there wasn't a speck of dust in sight. The old photo copiers, broken office furniture and recycling bins were gone. Now the room was filled with sunlight, comfy couches and an enormous L-shaped desk decorated with sports memorabilia.

"I never realized this room had so much space. It's twice the size of mine," she said, admiring the rich, sleek decor. She wanted to ask who the people were in the framed photographs on the wall, but decided against it. After all, they weren't friends and this wasn't a social call. "I see you've made yourself right at home."

"I plan to be here for awhile." Damien took off his jacket, inspected it, and dropped it behind his chair. "You spilled coffee on my suit. I'll send you the bill for my dry cleaning tomorrow."

Niveah rolled her eyes to the ceiling. "What did you want to talk to me about? I'm very busy, and I don't have time for idle chitchat."

He gestured for her to close the door, but when she didn't, he strode past her and slammed it. Damien liked the view from where he was standing so much, he decided against returning to his desk. Niveah had a sexy ass, great legs and a perfect set of boobs, so why was she dressed like a Hutterite woman? Did she think that downplaying her looks would help her clients take her more seriously? Before he could censor his thoughts, the question running through his mind burst out of his lips. "What's with the outfit?"

Niveah pivoted around on her heels. "Excuse me?"

"It's drab, dark and shapeless," he said, his gaze sliding down her hips. "It looks like something the hosts of that TLC makeover show would dump in the trash."

Now she was good and mad. Her chest was heaving, her

hands were clenched and when he stepped forward, she thought of kicking him in the shin.

Damien took another step.

There was no space between them now. If she sneezed he'd be covered in germs. The thought made a laugh bubble in her throat. It would serve Damien right for dissing her expensive suit. "Just because I have to work with you, doesn't mean I have to like you. Stay away from me and I'll be sure to do the same."

"Did you forget that I was summoned here to infuse life and creativity into your afflicted department?" He spoke in a conciliatory tone, but his righteous smile spoke of his pride. Damien Hunter thought he was "the man," and according to her misguided boss, he was. "There's no getting rid of me, Ms. Evans. I have a job to do and I'm going to do it. You feel me?"

Taking a deep breath didn't help Niveah relax. Neither did counting to ten. Or twenty. Damien was doing his damndest to piss her off and it was working. The man hadn't even been at Access Media and Entertainment for an hour, but she already hated his guts. *Why did I sleep with him?* she thought, overcome with regret. Guys like Damien Hunter were as common as an enchilada in Mexico, but she'd been too blinded by lust to realize it. "Let's call a truce. You stay on your side of the office and I'll stay on mine."

Aggressive women were a turn-on, and as Niveah advanced forward, he felt the impulse to kiss her. But when Damien remembered how their night ended on New Year's Eve, his interest waned. "Oh no you don't," he said, leaning against the door to prevent her escape. "We have some unfinished business to discuss. Once you answer my questions to *my* satisfaction, I'll be more than happy to let you go on your way."

Niveah stared at him, wondering why she'd ever found him attractive.

"Did you know who I was when you approached me at the hotel bar on Saturday night?" Damien continued before she had a chance to respond. "Think long and hard about your answer, because I have a knack for detecting bullshit."

His question didn't merit a response, but Niveah forced herself to answer. The sooner she got out of his office, the better. "If I had known you were the clown from the East Coast office I was being *forced* to work with, I wouldn't have wasted my best stuff on you."

Clown? Is that what everyone around the office referred to him as? "Don't flatter yourself, honey." He saw her eyes widen and couldn't resist adding, "I've had *much* better lovers."

A flush crept up Niveah's neck and over her cheeks.

"And while we're on the subject of our one-night stand, how much money did you get for my watch? Five, six grand?"

"Your watch? What makes you think I have that ugly knockoff?"

"Knockoff! Are you kidding me?" His strident tone drowned out the telephone ringing on his desk. "I don't wear cheap stuff. I only buy the best."

"I don't have your precious watch, so why don't you go ask one of the floozies who frequent your 'suite of love.' You know, those *much* better lovers you mentioned earlier."

Her tone, like her words, was filled with acrimony, and it took all of his self-control to keep from cursing. Damien was glad he didn't do relationships, because this saucy, pain in the ass woman was the type to drive him straight to the madhouse. Like his older sister, Niveah brought out the worst in him, and after five minutes in her presence he needed a stiff drink. "I never had anyone else in my room, so that leaves you as the culprit."

Damien promised himself he wasn't going to bring it up, wasn't going to think about it anymore, but the question burning in his mind slipped from between his lips before he could catch it. "Why did you creep out when I was in the shower?" He indulged in a sly, devilish grin. "Did things get too hot for you?"

"Quite the contrary." A smirk lit up her eyes. "I was, um, how do I put this nicely? I wasn't quite *satisfied* when you were done, so I went home to finish the job."

Her eyes sliced across his face, but it was her words that cut him deep. *She'd faked her orgasms?* The truth was more stunning than a blow to the head, and for a moment Damien was speechless. He needed time to absorb her words, to think things over, but unfortunately Niveah wasn't through with him yet.

"And one other thing…."

Proud she had reclaimed the upper hand, she launched a second, more explosive assault. "I've been with this company for ten years and I don't plan on going anywhere. I'm damn good at what I do, and no arrogant hotshot from New York is going to steal the VP position from me. *I* deserve this promotion, not you. But if you think you can compete with me, bring it on."

"Is that a challenge?"

"Most definitely."

"You have no idea what you're doing, *Ms. Evans.* I'll trample all over you."

"You're funny, Damien." Her smile was sweet, but her tone was ice. "When I'm named vice president in June, I think I just might let you keep your job. And this adorable little office."

Her mission accomplished, she strode past him and out the door with her head held high.

Damien's eyebrows shot up. This was the woman he was expected to work with on the Discreet Boutique ad campaign? Did someone have it out for him, or what! He felt drained, beaten down, as if he'd just had his ass kicked by a man twice his size. And it was all because of Niveah. A sister who looked like an angel but had a heart of stone.

It was a challenge, but Damien tried to look on the bright

side. At least she'd answered some of his questions. Their meeting on New Year's Eve had been a stroke of luck, not some elaborate scheme to blackmail him. But there was still the matter of her stealing his watch—and faking her orgasms. Was Niveah telling the truth or just trying to stick it to him?

His thoughts returned to the night in question. Damien could still hear her moans, still feel her thighs locked around his waist, still smell the scent of their fervent lovemaking. His desire for her was overwhelming, and for the first time in his life he'd put the needs of his lover above his own. To please her, he'd honored all of her requests. He'd stroked her vulva, kissed her clitoris, eagerly licked the rim of the swollen lips between her legs. Then, when she couldn't stand it anymore, he'd flipped her onto her stomach and plunged inside her with all his might.

"Faked an orgasm my ass," he grumbled, striding over to his desk and plopping onto his chair. He'd been with a lot of women in his life, but he'd never seen a woman lose control like that in bed. He didn't profess to be a stud between the sheets, but he refused to believe he hadn't pleased Niveah. Not when she'd been clawing his back, screaming his name, and begging for more. The sister was obviously emotionally unstable, and if he knew what was good for him, he'd stay the hell away from her.

To keep his mind off his argument with Niveah, Damien organized his office and finished unpacking the boxes he'd lugged in from his car hours earlier. The rest of the day flew by, and if one of the guys from the finance department hadn't stopped by to invite him for after-work drinks, he would have worked past quitting time.

The first thing Damien did when he walked into the upscale martini bar was scope out the lounge area for Niveah. She was nowhere to be found. He felt a pang of disappointment, but quickly stamped it out. Niveah Evans was the enemy, and he'd be wise to always remember that.

"Damien!"

"Hey, man, what's up!"

"Welcome to the team!"

Damien chuckled when he spotted his colleagues at one of the corner tables. As he strode through the bar, he retrieved his cell phone from his coat pocket. He had one message. Worried something might be wrong at home, he quickly punched in his password. He plugged his left ear with his index finger and turned away from the loud, gaily chattering patrons at the bar.

A woman with a pleasant voice identified herself as the assistant manager at the Ritz-Carlton hotel. "Earlier today, someone in the cleaning crew found your watch in suite 1284. We apologize for any distress this may have caused you, but it's available for pickup at the front desk of our downtown location. Mr. Hunter, if you have any questions or concerns, please don't hesitate to call me here at the hotel."

Damien deleted the message and shoved his cell phone back into his pocket. Damn. He'd accused Niveah of stealing his watch, but it had been back in his hotel suite all along. "A fine mess I've created this time," he grumbled, expelling a breath.

The right thing to do was to apologize, but Damien would rather eat a bowl of crickets than say "sorry" to the snotty creative director. Since Niveah hadn't apologized for skipping out on him on New Year's Eve, he wouldn't apologize for calling her a thief. An eye for an eye, right?

As he reached the table where his coworkers were sitting, a full-figured brunette wearing more makeup than a circus clown surged to her feet. "Mr. Hunter, take a load off. I saved you a seat right here beside me."

Reluctantly, he sat down in the vacant chair.

"How was your first day of work? Getting a feel for the place yet?" she asked, staring at him intently. "I can show you around tomorrow during my coffee break, if you'd like."

"No, thanks. If you've seen one photocopier, you've seen them all!"

The woman erupted in fake over-the-top giggles.

"Sir, what can I get you?"

Damien gave the waitress his order and listened with half an ear as his colleagues talked about their jobs, families and plans for the weekend. A popular country song came on, and the table quickly emptied, leaving Damien alone with one of the guys he'd met during lunch.

"Where's boss lady tonight? I expected her to be here, hanging out with the team."

"Niveah would never be caught dead in a place like this. This bar, like all of us, is beneath her." The computer specialist scrubbed at his pockmarked cheek. "But you'll see for yourself what a piece of work she is."

"She isn't that bad, is she?"

"Butter wouldn't melt in that woman's mouth," he snarled, a bitter expression on his tanned face. "What she needs is a good lay. If she had someone to rock her world on a regular basis, she wouldn't be such a raging bit—"

Damien gripped his arm. "Don't."

The fury in his tone must have shone through, because fear flashed in the man's eyes. "Sorry, you're right. That's no way to talk about a member of our team."

"Just don't let it happen again." Damien didn't like Niveah, and he suspected that everything the computer specialist said was true, but he hated hearing such a smart, successful woman being disrespected—even one he couldn't stand. "What's her story? Do you know much about her life outside of the office?"

"The office *is* her life. Niveah works evenings, weekends and has been known to come in on holidays, too." He paused to drink his beer. "She was engaged to a hotshot entertainment lawyer last year, but he broke things off just weeks before the wedding. No one knows for sure what happened, but there are rumors circulating that he had a chick on the side. Lucky bastard!"

The man chuckled, but Damien didn't.

"You know what I think? I think she's frigid in bed and her ex went looking for someone with a little more heat. Don't get me wrong, Niveah's a babe, but a woman has to be able to work it between the sheets, too."

And she most certainly can.

Dirty dancing had put Niveah in the mood, and when they kissed Damien felt a powerful rush of emotion. Frowning, he gave his head a hard shake. What had gotten into him? When had he become such a pansy? Keeping his cool around Niveah was paramount, but as he thought about their showdown that afternoon in his office, his doubts intensified. And if the rumors he'd heard about Niveah were true, it was going to be the longest eight weeks of his life. Eight hours on the job, and he already feared all hope was gone. He wasn't wearing plaid suspenders, and didn't have a squeaky voice, but whenever Niveah was around Damien felt like a pubescent kid, and that wasn't cool.

"I better get out of here. My fiancée's waiting on me." The guy stood, dropped a twenty-dollar bill on the table and grabbed his coat. "Good luck working with the Heart of Darkness."

Damien grabbed the neck of his beer bottle to keep from decking his colleague. Calling on every ounce of his self-control, he took a gulp of his beer. "Don't worry about me. I've been in this business a long time. I can hold my own against Ms. Evans."

"If you know what's good for you, you'll stay off of her bad side."

It's too late for that, Damien decided, shaking his head, *you should have warned me sooner.*

Chapter 5

The last two weeks had been filled with extreme highs and lows, and as Niveah prepared for the five-thirty brainstorming session, she wondered if the great Damien would be gracing the creative team with his presence. The man had more swagger than an Italian mobster and grated on her nerves every chance that he got. "I don't believe in working after hours," he'd said, three days earlier when she'd mentioned the meeting to him. "If you're having trouble getting your work done between nine and five, then you're mismanaging your time."

Niveah hadn't seen much of Damien today, but that didn't mean she hadn't thought about him. She had. In fact too much. He—not her numerous projects or responsibilities—filled her mind. The hallways held his scent, his laughter flowed out of his office and she'd spotted him at lunch chatting amicably with a group of interns.

To her surprise, Damien's presence had been felt immediately throughout Access Media and Entertainment.

The perfect combination of bad boy and southern gentleman, Damien had quickly become the life of the agency. He was the most arrogant, egocentric man to walk the face of the earth, but for some insane reason people liked him. Niveah couldn't go anywhere without someone mentioning his name. "Have you seen Mr. Hunter's swanky new office?" "Don't you love his red sports car?" and "Doesn't Damien look hot in his suit?"

Rolling her eyes had become Niveah's new favorite pastime, and as she recalled the heated debate she'd overheard during lunchtime, she let another one roll. George Clooney was the sexiest man alive, not Damien Hunter. She didn't care what anyone said. *Though Damien does have the sweetest, firmest lips I've ever tasted.*

At the same time the telephone buzzed, Mrs. Murphy poked her head into the doorway. "Ms. Evans, your mother is on line two." She started to turn away, then stopped. Her features were marred with apprehension. "Would it be all right if I left early today? My grandkids are taking me out for dinner tonight, and I'd like to go home and freshen up a bit."

"You can leave once you've typed up tomorrow's agenda." Niveah placed her hand on the phone. "And don't forget to make a hundred copies of the market research file before you go. Everyone on the team needs to review it tonight."

Mrs. Murphy nodded, her mouth a tight, hard line. "Yes, Ms. Evans."

"Hi, Mom." Cradling the phone against her shoulder and her ear, she continued typing her report. "I heard on the news that it's been raining there all week. Are you and Dad all right?"

"We're fine. Bubba Maclean—you know, that tall, strapping boy who lives on the corner with his grandparents—was kind enough to come by and fix the screen door. The wind all but blew it off its hinges. Thankfully, the storm let up this afternoon."

Thunder boomed, drawing Niveah's attention away from her computer screen and out the window. Large, muddy puddles dotted Main Street and women in high heels tiptoed precariously around them. Niveah stared outside absently, her thoughts a million miles away. It seemed to be raining everywhere, and the reports she'd heard on the news made her wonder how her parents were really faring in Chickasaw. A year ago she'd paid for their home to receive extensive renovations, but it hadn't helped much. The three-bedroom bungalow was on its last legs, and until she landed the vice president position, there was little she could do about it. "Mom, did you get the money I sent you?"

"Yes, honey, and it was more than enough. Thank you."

Niveah heard the distant sound of dogs howling, and knew her mother was outside on the porch. In the evenings, her mom liked to sit in her rocking chair, sipping sweet tea. Sometimes she'd knit, other times she'd poke around in the garden. Even after all these years, Niveah could still smell the scent of fresh cucumbers wafting on the humid, summer breeze.

"Norma-Jean, you take such good care of us," Mrs. Evans said in her distinct southern twang. "Sometimes I don't know what we'd do without you."

Niveah cringed at the sound of her birth name. God, she hated it. The first thing she'd done when she'd left Chickasaw fifteen years ago was legally change her name, and despite showing her parents the documentation, they still didn't believe her. "Mom, it's Niveah, remember?"

"You can change your name, jazz up your look and move halfway around the world, but you'll always be plain ole' Norma-Jean to us."

Lucky me, she thought sourly. "Where's Dad?"

"He just left to go play his numbers, but I'll get him to call you when he gets back," she promised. "I thought I'd ring you up to share some exciting news."

A frown crimped Niveah's lips. The last time her mom had

called to share some "exciting news," she'd ended up footing the bill for her eighteen-year-old cousin, Josie, to go on a class trip to the state capital. "What's up, Mom?"

"Your father and I are coming to Tampa!"

What? The telephone slipped out of Niveah's hand, and fell on the desk with a thump. Her stomach coiled into knots, then flopped and plunged headfirst to her feet.

"Honey, are you still there?"

Niveah swiped up the phone. Seconds passed. And still, she didn't speak. English was her first language, and she didn't have a learning disability, but she didn't understand what her mother was saying. "That's great news," she choked out. "What are you coming down here for?"

"To see you, of course! You haven't been home in ages, honey, and we miss you. Five years is a long time to go without seeing your only child."

Niveah's thoughts were all over the place, scrambled, like one of those thousand-piece puzzles she liked doing on Sunday afternoons, but she managed to say, "Mom, I'd love to see you and Dad, but now's not a good time. I'm in the middle of a monster business deal, and—"

"That's what you said last year and the year before that," she huffed, her tone taking on a bitter edge. "At this rate, the next time we'll be together is at my funeral!"

"Mom, don't say things like that."

"It's true, and you know it," Mrs. Evans snapped. "I don't want to hear another word about it. We're coming to see you in April, and that's final. I'll call you next week to let you know what date and time we'll be at the depot."

Niveah stared down at the phone as if her mom was speaking Pig Latin. "Mom, that's a long trip for you and Dad to make by bus. You're looking at two or three days to get here," she pointed out. "In a few weeks, things will settle down around the office, and we can plan a family trip somewhere real nice. What do you say?"

Her question was met with silence.

"I'll have to talk to your father about it."

"You guys discuss it, and I'll call you over the weekend, okay?"

"Sure, honey."

Niveah heard the sadness and despair in those two little words, and felt three inches tall. "I love you, Mom. Give Dad my best."

The line disconnected, and Niveah slowly replaced the receiver. Guilt troubled her conscience. She shouldn't have dissuaded her mom from coming to town. Not when they were the sole reason for her success. If not for them pinching pennies and saving every dollar they earned at their minimum-wage jobs, she'd still be in Chickasaw working at the local thrift store.

Niveah sighed deeply, her conversation with her mom weighing heavily on mind. It wouldn't be so bad if her parents came to visit her for a few days, would it? She'd put them up in an expensive hotel, show them around the city and spoil them the way they deserved.

"What are you thinking about in that pretty little head of yours?"

Heat burned Niveah's cheeks. Embarrassed that Damien— the person she hated more than the kid who'd tormented her relentlessly in the fifth grade—had caught her staring off into space, she averted her gaze. "What do you want?" Niveah hoped her tone conveyed her disgust; but in case it didn't, she glared at him. "I have a tight deadline, and I don't have time for—"

"Idle chitchat," he finished, looking pleased with himself. "You're so predictable."

Watching him over the rim of her glasses, Niveah grudgingly conceded to herself that Damien Hunter was one fine man. Smartly dressed in a dark, tailored suit, and an eye-catching plum-colored tie, it was hard not to stare at him.

"Don't you own anything besides stuffy, black suits?" His gaze slipped down her chest. "Access Media is a vibrant, exciting company, but every day you show up to work looking like a pissed-off funeral director."

Niveah tugged at the sleeve of her blazer. What was Damien's problem? Why was he always making snide comments about her clothes? Niveah shot daggers at him, and felt vindicated when a streak of guilt flashed across his face. She had half a mind to report him to Human resources for…for…what? Critiquing her wardrobe? Banishing the absurd thought, she folded her arms rigidly across her chest. "Damien. What. Do. You. Want?"

"I want to know why you look nothing like the woman I met at the Ritz-Carlton two weeks ago, and more like a—"

"I don't have time to talk about fashion trends with you right now." Niveah swept a hand across her desk. "As you can see, I'm incredibly busy."

"I'm leaving for the day, and just wanted to remind you to fax the Discreet Boutique budget to me at home when you're done looking it over."

Niveah knew it was five o'clock, but made a point of staring down at her watch. "You start late and leave early. What a nice setup. No wonder you like it here so much."

His eyes disappeared behind a glare, but when he spoke his voice was free of anger. "I understand that you've planned another brainstorming session for tonight." Damien closed her door and advanced into her office. "You know what I think? I think you purposely schedule these meetings after hours to exclude me."

The scarf around Niveah's neck felt as if it was choking her. Unfortunately, fussing with it didn't help to loosen the knot in her throat. "That's ridiculous," she argued, shifting around on her chair. "Why would I do that?

"I don't know. You tell me."

Another step forward.

Niveah's hands were trembling, but she managed to flip open her daily planner. "If it makes you happy, I can reschedule the brainstorming session to Friday morning at eight a.m."

"That's too early. I don't clock in until nine."

Niveah made a face. And he did, too. He looked large and in charge and drop-dead sexy. His black leather briefcase gave him a powerful, distinguished air, one she was incredibly attracted to. Her eyes moved down his body, and although she was seated behind her desk a good five feet away from Damien, she felt vulnerable, exposed, as if he could see through her blouse.

There was that familiar pull again. That strong, overwhelming urge to kiss him. Her body yearned for him, and there wasn't a damn thing she could do about it.

"You don't have to do this, you know."

At the sound of Damien's voice, Niveah snapped out of her thoughts. "What are you talking about? I don't have to do what?"

"Work twelve hour days, seven days a week." A thoughtful expression warmed his face. "Everyone around here knows what a great creative director you are. You don't have to try and impress us. We got it. You're the best."

"I love what I do, Damien. I don't know why that's so hard for you to believe."

"President Obama doesn't work as much as you do!"

His joke didn't draw laughs.

"Life is a lot more than creating print ads and commercials. It's about trying new things, taking risks and living by the seat of your pants."

"You've got *that* department covered." Niveah eased forward in her chair, her gaze locked intently on his face. "You've made enough friends here for the both of us. That's why you're always rushing out of here early, so you can party the night away with all the single women on staff."

Niveah winced when she saw a grin light the corners of Damien's mouth. The expression on his face was one of pride. *Great, because of my snide comment he thinks I'm jealous. What an absurd notion.* If she had the power, she would turn back the hands of time. Instead of approaching Damien at the Ritz-Carlton, she would have gone home, changed into her pj's, and watched Dick Clark alone.

Liar. You wouldn't change a damn thing about that night, and you know it.

"To be successful in this business you have to put the time in, and if you're not willing to sacrifice your personal life you'll never make it to the top." Niveah cast her eyes back over her agenda. "The big presentation is fast approaching, and we don't have much time to put everything together. I'd feel better if we decided on a slogan tonight, and spent the next few days tying up loose ends."

"I'll need a few minutes to make some calls."

"By all means, use my phone."

He held up his BlackBerry. "No thanks, I have my cell."

"Okay, I'll meet you in the conference room in ten minutes."

"You do that." His grin widened as he turned toward the door. "And whatever you do, Niveah, don't keep me waiting."

Someone—likely Damien—had taken the liberty of ordering in Chinese food, and now the entire conference room smelled like wonton soup. Empty containers lined the refreshment table and the scent of alcohol was heavy in the air. Niveah suspected the plastic cups her employees were clutching were filled with more than just fruit punch. And she blamed Damien. This was not how she ran her evening brainstorming sessions. The rules were simple: no food, no drinks and no cell phones. Mr. Russo had stopped her in the hall to talk, and when she'd finally arrived at the meeting, everyone was already chowing down. What was she supposed to do? Rip the spring rolls out of peoples' hands and toss them into the trash?

Angry at herself for inviting Damien in the first place, she released a deep, heavy sigh. The brainstorming session had turned into a gabfest, and as she listened to a junior ad executive share another dimwitted idea, thoughts of killing Damien and hiding his body in the storage room filled her mind.

"The Discreet Boutique ad campaign will be a hit as long as it has babes, beer and cars. That's all men really care about, and the more of it we have in the spot the better," explained the kid with the unruly brown hair. "This is what we should do…"

Tuning out the speaker, Niveah aimed her eyes at the back of the room. She felt a rush of desire. Damien was standing in front of the whiteboard, cup in hand, jotting down ideas. After eating, he'd shed his suit jacket, loosened his tie and rolled up his sleeves. Confidence was sexy and she enjoyed watching Damien in his element. He was the center of attention— cracking jokes, keeping the mood light, ensuring everyone's ideas were heard.

Her eyes slid down his fit body. Not only was Damien amazing to look at, he was full of life and personality. She'd never admit it to anyone, but what she admired most about him was how effortlessly he connected with people. Damien had pull, star power, that indescribable quality that rock stars possessed in spades. Then there was his mouth, his thick lips and his broad shoulders. And below the belt he was— Niveah pressed her eyes shut. If she wanted to make it through the rest of the brainstorming session she had to focus. No more thoughts of Damien. Besides, she was supposed to be thinking of a catchy slogan for Discreet Boutique's menswear line, not fantasizing about the sexy New Yorker.

"Let's do this," a marketing intern proposed, spreading his

hands across an invisible TV screen. "Put a guy on a beach, surround him with a dozen bikini models and—"

Niveah had had enough. If she didn't take control of this meeting they'd never get the presentation done. "That'll never work." All heads swiveled in her direction. Niveah knew it was rude to interrupt, but she couldn't help herself. The intern was babbling, and his idea made about as much sense as buying a pregnancy test from the dollar store. "You've come up with a lot of stupid ideas over the months, Latrelle, but that has to be the worst one to date. Your concept has nothing to do with the product, and it's as cliché as they come. We need something fresh and exciting to kick off this campaign, not something that's been done to death."

Damien abandoned the whiteboard, and stood behind the Snoop Dog lookalike. "All Latrelle is saying is to keep the ads simple. You don't need a lot fanfare to capture a guy's interest, so don't overdo it. Just let the menswear line sell itself."

"Thanks, Mr. Hunter." Latrelle's grin returned as he draped a bony arm over the back of his chair. "Filling the ad with babes will definitely create a lot of buzz."

Protests erupted from the women in the room.

"Parading scantily-clad females around on a beach is not only tacky, it's degrading."

"You're not backing his idea, are you, Mr. Hunter?"

"I thought you had *way* more class than that."

Niveah wanted to cheer. Damien had his head in a noose now. Finally her colleagues would see for themselves what a sexist the smooth-tongued creative director was. *Let's see how he talks himself out of this one!* she thought, growing excited.

"I for one am sick of seeing females exploited in the media, and I refuse to be a part of another beer-type ad campaign," fumed Melody Scott, wearing a scowl that would frighten a UFC fighter. "Damien, maybe that's how you operate at

Access Media and Entertainment in New York, but we pride ourselves on being classy in this office."

Ouch. Niveah stared on in shock as Melody berated all of the men in the room Glen Beck style. Every time Damien tried to speak, she raised her voice, effectively drowning out his rebuttal. For a split second, Niveah considered coming to Damien's defense. No, that was a bad idea. Damien was a big boy; he could handle himself.

Damien had never been so incensed, and as he listened to Melody berate him, all the muscles tightened in his jaw and neck. Tired of standing, and convinced the marketing associate was going to talk until the second coming of Christ, he returned to his seat, fuming. The walls were closing in, making Damien feel as if he was trapped inside of a prison cell.

Tapping his fingers on the table, Damien replayed the last ten minutes of the discussion in his mind. He still couldn't believe Melody had called him sexist. And in front of Niveah no less. The woman had no right jumping down his throat. He was simply making a point, and given her proclivity for tight, revealing clothes, he was surprised by her over-the-top reaction. *She's a fine one to talk about women's rights!*

Damien glanced at Niveah. He hated her drab business suits, but at least she always looked classy and well put together. *What the hell?* His ears perked up when Melody suggested he take a course in female sensitivity.

"Thank you, Melody, for so adequately stating your point, but I'd like a chance to clarify my previous statement." Damien spoke calmly, but he was angrier than a raging bull. Prepared to do war, he stood and returned to the whiteboard. "As you can see from the notes I've made tonight, the most profitable commercials made within the last ten years combined sexuality, humor and elements of pop culture. I wasn't suggesting we have bikini models just the sake of it; but if it fits with the theme and tone of the ad, I'm all for it, because at the end of the day it isn't about our personal preferences, it's about what will sell."

Tension brewed, swirling around the room like an invisible tornado.

Melody snorted in disdain. "Fine, but I want it duly noted that I'm not in agreement with a sexist ad that objectifies women. I have a reputation to protect, one that I refuse to have tainted."

"We all want to succeed," Damien replied smoothly, "and we need each other to make it happen. I want to create a kick-ass campaign for Discreet Boutiques, but I can't do it without each and every one of you."

"I'm behind you a hundred percent!" someone yelled from across the room.

"Me, too!" another said. "What do you want me to do?"

Damien smiled. Order had been restored, and now his colleagues were buzzing with excitement. "Albert, log onto your laptop and do a search on…"

Niveah caught his eye, and for a moment Damien forgot what he was going to say. He recovered, outlined what he wanted the graphic designer to do, and took a moment to catch his breath. Resting on the edge of the table, he reached for his folder of notes on Discreet Boutique, Incorporated. Damien pretended to be perusing the file, but he was actually watching Niveah on the sly. He saw her undo her blazer and felt his jimmy spring to life. She was wearing a gray blouse, and although Damien hated the color he liked that it showed some cleavage. It was the most skin he'd seen from Niveah in weeks, and seeing her creamy brown flesh made him want to lick from her ears to her breasts.

Damien ran his index finger along the inside of his shirt collar. Swallowing hard didn't remove the lump in his throat. His breathing grew deep, labored, as if he'd just finished the last leg of a triathlon. Damien had always considered himself cool, but tonight he felt like Pavlov's dog. All he needed now was a collar and a leash. Niveah couldn't move a muscle without him getting an erection. It was pathetic the way he was eying her, but he couldn't stop. He ached to love her, please her, taste the sweet treasure between her legs just one more time.

Giving his head a good, hard shake helped clear his thoughts. Before he did something that would land him in the human resource director's office for sexual harassment, he brought the brainstorming session to a close. "All right, folks. That will be all for tonight."

The room emptied in seconds and quiet descended. Damien massaged his neck, hoping to alleviate the pain radiating up his shoulders. From where he was standing, he could see Niveah in the hall talking to one of their colleagues. Her back was to him, giving him a clear view of her sexy derriere. Thinking about how she'd ground her ass into his crotch when they were cuddling in bed made him burn with lust.

A grin claimed Damien's lips. That had been one hell of a night. And he'd been unable to think of anything else ever since. He wondered if Niveah had a hard time forgetting New Year's Eve, too. Was she bombarded with sexual images every moment of the day? Or had she moved on to someone else? Women like Niveah were single by choice, often choosing their careers over marriage and having babies, and knowing that no one had claims on her gave Damien hope. Maybe, if he was lucky, they could turn their one-night stand into more evenings filled with passionate, earth-shattering sex?

At the thought his heart raced. He'd been with a lot of women, everyone from models to singers and dancers, but no one had captured his attention like Niveah. He couldn't put his finger on it, but there was something about the creative director he found irresistible. It was that indescribable quality that made it impossible for him to forget her.

Damien opened his briefcase and chucked files inside. Tonight, he'd discovered a startling truth. Fighting against his attraction to Niveah was as pointless as running backward. His desire for her couldn't be denied or contained, and the more he tried to ignore it, the more powerful it was. *I've had her once, and I'll have her again,* he decided, tossing his suit jacket over his shoulders. *And, I know just what to do to make it happen.*

Chapter 6

"Hold the elevator!"

Niveah's heart plunged to the elevator floor. She'd recognize that deep, husky voice in her sleep, and when a hand reached out and pried open the elevator door, the knot in her throat threatened to suffocate her. Forcing a smile, she acknowledged Damien's presence with a curt nod. He'd thwarted her clean getaway, but Niveah refused to stress over being alone with him. If she could deliver the keynote address at the annual advertising conference in Brazil last year, then she could certainly handle a ten-second ride with Damien.

"Thanks. This old thing takes forever to reach the lobby, and I'm in a hurry."

All the muscles in her body tensed. His scent was bold and sophisticated, and when it fell over her, images of being back in his executive suite at the Ritz-Carlton filled her mind. Shutting her eyes didn't ward off the memories.

Underneath her blouse her nipples hardened. What was the matter with her? Why couldn't she move past it? Every time

Damien was around she relived their night together. Every passionate minute of it. It was frustrating, but there didn't seem to be a damn thing she could do about it. To distance herself from her lewd, sexual thoughts, Niveah stared intently at the elevator floor lights. 24…23…22…

"Where are you rushing off to?" Damien asked, turning toward her. "You're always the last one to leave the office, but tonight you raced out of the conference room before everyone else. Do you have a hot date tonight? A late-night hookup or something?"

Offended, she flung an angry look at him. What was he implying? That she was a nymphomaniac on the prowl for someone to screw?

"I'm sorry. That didn't come out right." His smile slid away and he wore a sympathetic expression. "I didn't mean to offend you."

"I don't have any plans. I'm just anxious to get home." Niveah didn't want to prolong the conversation, but curiosity pushed her to ask. "What are you up to this weekend?"

Leaning against the wall, his eyes sparkling with mischief, Damien looked both tempting and sexy. "I haven't decided yet. I might hang out with friends, catch a movie at the new Cineplex Dome up in Westchase or play indoor hockey."

Niveah forced her legs to stop shaking. Shifting her feet, she tightened her already fierce grip on her briefcase. Damien was standing too close, staring at her too intently and making her feel more uncomfortable than a drug dealer in church.

"Are you free tomorrow evening?"

Before she could decline, he told her that Mrs. Garrett-Reed was arriving from Minneapolis tomorrow and he had made dinner reservations at the Acropolis Greek tavern. "Mr. Russo will be joining us as well. If you're interested, I can call and have your name added to the list."

Confused, Niveah raised an eyebrow. "That's strange. I

spoke at length with Mr. Russo this afternoon and he never mentioned that Mrs. Garrett-Reed was coming to town."

"It probably slipped his mind. He's as astute as they come, but he *is* sixty-two."

"I wonder what this is all about. Our meeting with Discreet Boutiques isn't until the end of the month." Niveah considered one scenario after another. Something had to be wrong. Why else would Mrs. Garrett-Reed be coming to town? "What time does she arrive?"

"At four o'clock, why"

"I wish I'd known sooner. If I had, I wouldn't have made plans with my girlfriends." Once a month, Niveah, Jeanette and Roxi spent the day together, catching up on each other's busy lives. Cancelling would guarantee a blow-out with Roxi, and Niveah wasn't in the mood to get into a verbal sparring match with her friend. "I would have loved to show Mrs. Garrett-Reed around Tampa. This is her first time here, and I want it to be special for her."

"Don't worry, I've got it covered."

"No offense, Damien, but you're not from around here. Only a native would know to skip all the tourist spots, and go to—"

"The open market in Ybor City, the fun expo in Madison and to Olive's Clef for lunch. I live for their half-pound T-bone steaks. Their cream and mushroom sauce is out of this world."

Niveah gave him a sideways glance. How did Damien know about her favorite out-of-the-way spots? "I don't know why I'm surprised," she wondered out loud. "You're the type who gets around, so it's no wonder you know where all of the coolest places are in the city."

A big, broad, ear-to-ear grin claimed his mouth.

To create some space, Niveah took a giant step backward. It was either put some distance between them, or do what she'd been fantasizing about doing for weeks—kissing him senselessly. Heat crept up the back of Niveah's neck as the scene played out in her mind. Throwing herself at Damien would not only tarnish her reputation, it would put her career in jeopardy. And she'd worked too damn hard to throw everything away.

"It probably isn't safe for us to be in here." His eyes slid down her face and lingered on the curve of her hips. "You remember what happened the last time we were alone, don't you?"

Why hadn't they reached the lobby yet? Niveah thought, as panic flooded through her. *Oh, God, the damn thing is broken! That's why it's moving at a snail's pace!*

"These days, I can't get into an elevator without thinking about you. It's been three weeks, but I can still hear your moans of pleasure."

"That was a long time ago."

"Too long if you ask me." He smoothed a hand over his goatee, his head cocked to the left as if cogitating over a complex algebra equation. "What about a do-over?"

Fear prevented Niveah from speaking. She didn't mind a little harmless flirting, but now Damien had gone too far. "We agreed not to discuss what happened on New Year's Eve," she reminded him, trying valiantly not to stare at his mouth. Three weeks ago, she'd licked it, kissed it, sucked it as if it was coated in dark chocolate. "Leave that night in the past where it belongs."

Damien moved closer. His eyes teased, glistened, twinkled with lust and desire.

It was impossible not to want him, but she had to be strong—had to remember that Damien was the ultimate lady killer, a man who lived for the thrill of the chase. He was as personable as he was charming, a self-professed master at seduction.

"I haven't been able to stop thinking about that night, have you?"

A squeak rose up in her throat. Her head was throbbing, and Niveah worried that she might faint. Or worse, act on her impulses. It wasn't easy sharing a small, confined space with a man who pulsed with sexual energy. If they were back in the office it would be easy to distance herself from him, but in the elevator there was nowhere to hide.

Niveah took a long, deep breath. Damien made her hyperventilate, and her vision was so hazy she couldn't make out the numbers being lit up at each floor.

"The only way to overcome our attraction for each other is to face it head-on."

His hand caressed her arm so lightly Niveah thought she'd imagined it. Damien drew her to him. Staring into his eyes only intensified her need. Her lips were dry, her nipples yearned for his tongue and her panties were soaking wet. Never before had she wanted a man this much. Her desire for him was great, tremendous, more explosive than gasoline-laced dynamite.

"I've had my fair share of women, but this thing between us is different." He lowered his head until their foreheads were touching. "I'm trying to fight my attraction to you, but it just keeps getting stronger."

Damien crushed his mouth against hers. The kiss was packed with so much heat Niveah went limp in his arms. She ran a hand over his chest, and purred when he sucked her lips into his mouth. His kiss was impatient, aggressive, and when he pressed her against the wall, she clung to him to keep from falling. Damien fiddled with the buttons on her jacket. Niveah didn't even try to stop him. Everything that had happened over the last month had led them to this point. The sly glances, the quips, the jokes. It was inevitable that they were going to cross the line again, but Niveah never imagined it would happen in an elevator.

"Damn, baby. You feel amazing. Better than I remember," he confessed, pressing his lips against the curve of her ear.

Damien cupped her butt, ground his erection into her. "I can't wait to get you out of these clothes. Every time you crossed your legs during the meeting I lost my mind. I wanted to bend you over the conference room table and plunge so deep inside you…"

At the mention of the evening brainstorming session, reason kicked in. And just like that, the spell Damien had over her was broken. She pulled out of his arms and reclaimed her briefcase lying on the floor. "The next time you force yourself on me, I'll file a sexual harassment complaint with the human resources department." Her voice was thin, but she pressed on. "We are colleagues, and you need to act like such at all times."

"I didn't force myself on you. You were feeling that kiss just as much as I was."

"I was in shock. I didn't know what was happening." Niveah lowered her eyes. Thank God she'd come to her senses in time. Making love to Damien on New Year's Eve had been the most exciting thing to ever happen to her, but she wasn't willing to throw her career away for a night of passion. Not even with a man she shared an insane sexual chemistry with.

"Do you expect me to believe that you're not attracted to me? That you don't want me as much as I want you?" His voice oozed with contempt, but the expression on his face was somber. "I'm offering you a night of physical pleasure with no emotions involved. What could be better than that?"

He put his hands on the wall, fencing her in.

Niveah tensed. She wanted to move away, but lacked the willpower. Weakened by his kiss, she tried to ignore the glorious tingling sensation spreading through her core. "If you touch me again, I'll have you written up for sexual misconduct."

"You wouldn't."

Niveah lifted her chin. "Try me."

A beat passed, then Damien called her bluff. He lowered his

mouth until it was just inches away from her lips. His cologne swept over her like a scented breeze, and at that moment Niveah realized she didn't have a ghost of a chance getting out of the elevator with her dignity intact. She wanted him more than she'd ever wanted anyone, and they both knew it.

"I've never been one to resist a challenge," he confessed, his gaze creeping down her hips. "One day, I'll take you up on that very tempting offer, but for now we'll play by your rules."

The elevator pinged then creaked to a halt on the ground floor.

Niveah exhaled as relief flooded through her. *Free at last, free at last, thank God Almighty, I'm free at last!* She stepped forward, but Damien slid over to the right, blocking her path. "I don't have time to play games. I really have to go."

"I'll see you tomorrow night at Acropolis. Six o'clock sharp. Wear a dress and leave your hair down; I'm tired of seeing it in that homely bun."

"Anything else, oh controlling one?"

"I'd love another kiss."

For the second time that night, desire overpowered her. Niveah felt her lips part, and her head tilt. What happened to resisting him? To being strong in the face of this gorgeous, six-foot-plus roadblock? There was only one explanation for her uncharacteristic behavior: Damien must have put a spell on her. Or slipped something into her coffee when she wasn't looking. Why else would she consider having sex with him at the expense of her career?

Determined to remain strong, Niveah struck down the thought and snapped out of her haze. Damien wasn't in charge of her body, she was. But the predatory look in his eyes told a different story. He was going to have her, and there was nothing she could do about it. A fresh wave of fear rushed through her. Scared her resolve would weaken, she bolted out of the elevator, desperate to put space between her and the man who'd haunted her dreams for the last month.

"Where are we going?" Niveah asked, peering out the passenger window of Jeanette's black compact car. It had been raining all morning, resulting in heavier than normal traffic and clogged side streets. "This isn't the way to Ellenton outlet mall."

Jeanette made a left turn at the next intersection. "We go shopping all the time. I thought we could do something that stimulates the mind as well as the body."

"Yay! We're going to the spa!" Roxi's face brightened. "I don't know about you two, but I need to unwind in the worst way."

Isn't that the truth, Niveah thought, remembering what happened yesterday in the elevator with Damien. It had taken two chilled glasses of wine to extinguish the fire his kiss had caused, and when she finally slipped into bed and closed her eyes, she saw his face smiling back at her. The man made her weak, and the more she resisted him the more her desire grew. Bolting from the elevator had saved her from making the biggest mistake of her career, but she couldn't help wondering what would've happened if she'd taken Damien up on his offer.

"We're here," Jeanette announced.

Niveah peered through the rain-streaked windshield and groaned. "What are we doing at Outrageously Fit? You know how much I hate exercising."

"I know, but my brother's girlfriend teaches the hot yoga class, and it's awesome."

"I've been wanting to check this place out for weeks," Roxi said, unbuckling her seat belt. "Since you have a membership the session is free right?"

Jeanette nodded. "Let's go. It starts in ten minutes and I want to be up front."

Niveah complained as they dashed across the parking lot. Inside, pop music, high-pitched laughter and grunts filled the air. The weight room overflowed with muscle men, perfect-looking women sweated it out on various exercise machines and exasperated mothers dragged screaming children out of the playroom. "I wish you'd told me this was what you had in mind," Niveah yelled over the music. "If I had known I would have gone to the office."

Roxi sucked her teeth. "Do you have to talk about work every second of every day?"

"If you knew how much pressure I was under, you wouldn't be asking me that."

"Don't even start, you two." Jeanette handed the lady at the desk her membership card, then beckoned her friends to follow. "Come on. The room is this way."

Niveah followed behind Roxi like an ox going to the butcher. She admired her friend's quest for personal health and wellness, but she had absolutely no interest in doing headstands. She had dinner plans for six o'clock, and showing up at the best restaurant in Tampa in a neck brace wouldn't be cute.

"I'm so glad you could make it," a trim blonde said, throwing her arms around Jeanette. "Find a spot, grab a mat and stretch really well. Contrary to what people think, yoga isn't easy, and I'd hate for one of you to pull a muscle."

The instrumental music and vanilla-scented incense instantly calmed Niveah. Maybe this yoga thing wasn't so bad, she thought, plunking onto her mat. For the next hour, she didn't have to think about work or her feelings for Damien, and that was a very good thing.

Niveah closed her eyes. Instead of concentrating on her breathing, she went over everything that happened on New Year's Eve. Meeting Damien at the bar, their sensual dance, returning to his suite and making love until they passed out from exhaustion.

How many more times was she going to relive their night together? Making love had never mattered to her before. A couple times a month had always been enough, but now she was fantasizing about doing the nasty every five minutes. When had she become obsessed with sex?

Since you met Damien, a voice said.

It was true. He had some kind of hold on her and Niveah didn't know how to overcome it. From the moment she spotted him at the Ritz-Carlton bar, she'd been taken by him. And seeing him at work day after day only increased her desire. What woman wouldn't lust after a dark, gorgeous man who'd pleased her in bed?

"Jeanette, what time does the comedy showcase start tonight?"

"Doors open at seven, but we should probably be there an hour early if we want good seats."

"About that," Niveah began, breaking free of her thoughts. "I can't go with you guys to the comedy showcase tonight."

Roxi adjusted her ponytail. "Why, do you have plans with that fine-ass New Yorker?"

Niveah fumbled over her words, and her girlfriends squealed.

"I knew something was going on!" Jeanette practically leapt onto her best friend. "And I'm not the only one. Girl, you're leading in the office pool! Initially, I thought Essence Jackson would be the one to snag Damien, but when I saw you two in the staff room a few days ago, all hugged up by the watercooler, I knew ya'll were hot for each other."

"First of all, we weren't all 'hugged up' in the staff room. Damien was showing me the brief for the internet ad he's working on, and I was merely making notes on the file."

Jeanette winked. "Sure you were. Don't worry, sisterfriend. Your secret is safe with me."

"It's not a date, you guys. Mr. Russo and Mrs. Garrett-Reed will be there, too."

"I think it's great that you've finally put that mess with Stewart behind you and found someone else. You and Damien make a striking couple, and I bet the sex is off the charts."

"You know, you never did tell us what went down on New Year's Eve." Roxi studied Niveah closely. "Is Damien packing like a plumber or a member of the itty-bitty club?"

Niveah knew that her response would incite another raucous outburst, but she didn't care. Making love to Damien had been the best sexual experience of her life, and she wanted the world to know. "Let's just say that he's been *very* blessed below the belt."

"Well, I'll be damned..." Roxi put her index finger in her mouth and bit down on her nail. "After you finish with him tonight, can you send him over to my house?"

Laughter sputtered out of Jeanette's mouth. "A few weeks ago you said Cedrick was the love of your life, and now you're ready to replace him. What's up with that?"

"Cedrick's too old for me."

Niveah and Jeanette shared a puzzled look. "But you're the same age."

"Exactly, *that's* the problem."

Jeanette scratched the side of her head. "Roxi, I don't understand. You're not making any sense. Why is Cedrick's age an issue all of a sudden?"

"Because he won't go down on me. Can you believe it? It's the twenty-first century, but Cedrick's ass is still stuck in the eighteen hundreds."

Jeanette held up her hands. "Hold on. Let me get this straight. You're breaking up with Cedrick because he's not performing the way you want in bed? Sex isn't everything, and—"

"Oh yes it is!"

"Be reasonable," Niveah advised. "Cedrick's a good man and he thinks the world of you."

"Right, that's why he called me selfish and immature last

night in bed." Scowling, her eyebrows merged at the apex of her nose and she gave a snort of disgust. "Did you know that women hit their sexual peak at forty, while men lose interest in sex as they age? That means in a couple years when I'm hitting my stride, Cedrick will be throwing in the towel!"

Jeanette scooted over on her mat, bringing her shoulder-to-shoulder with Niveah. "Let's get back to your date with Damien. What are you going to wear? And please don't tell me one of your boring black business suits."

"Spare me the lecture. I've had about enough of everyone giving me fashion tips."

"I'll quit giving you advice once you stop hiding that gorgeous body under dull work clothes."

"Flirt like crazy tonight," Roxi encouraged. "Male attention is good for the soul. It makes me feel sexy and alive and as desirable as a Bond girl!"

Jeanette nodded fervently. "And don't bore him all night by talking about work."

"Successful men always travel in packs, so stop being greedy and hook me up with one of Damien's rich, hot friends." Roxi laughed. "Just make sure he's *under* thirty!"

"I'm going to say this one more time. In no way, shape or form am I interested in Damien Hunter. He's the most obnoxious man I've ever met and I'm starting to hate his arrogant guts."

"Niveah, I didn't just meet you," Jeanette said, patting her on the leg. "I've known you for years and I can tell that you like Damien, so stop fighting your feelings for him and let the chips fall where they may!"

The instructor took her place in front of the group. "Okay everyone. It's time to get started. We're going to begin today's session by doing some simple stretching exercises. This will help loosen up your body and…"

"Wear that blue Gucci dress with the plunging neckline

tonight," Jeanette advised, flashing a thumbs-up sign. "Damien won't be able to keep his hands off you."

Niveah swallowed. *That's what I'm afraid of.*

Chapter 7

Glad to be the first one to arrive at the Acropolis Greek tavern, Niveah followed the maitre d' through the restaurant. Once seated at the corner table beside the window, she admired the eclectic Mediterranean decor. Bronze statues stood at the entrance of the dining area, chandeliers loomed overhead and Greek music was playing softly.

Niveah drew her fingers over her chain-link necklace. It was either that or adjust her dress for the hundredth time. Instead of selecting the tight, eye-catching outfit Jeanette had suggested, she'd gone with something safe. Something chic and sophisticated, that wouldn't draw any unwanted attention from Damien or anyone else.

Her heart was racing fast, beating out of control. Niveah didn't know if she was nervous about seeing Damien again or…no, that was it. Kissing him yesterday in the elevator had changed the dynamics of their relationship, and deep down she feared what he would do next. What if he kissed her again? Was she strong enough to resist him a second time?

Worried her nerves would get the best of her, she took a sip from her water glass. A shadow fell across the table, and Niveah glanced to her left.

Three teenagers dressed in identical suits and red bow ties were staring at her. "Ma'am, are you presently satisfied with your internet provider?" the tallest of the young men queried. "Did you know that Net Zero was voted number one in customer satisfaction, service fees and online technical support?"

Niveah discreetly searched the room for a waiter but came up empty. Where was the maitre d'? Wasn't it his job to keep solicitors out of the restaurant?

"Do you know why more customers choose Net Zero than any other internet provider?"

"No, but I have a feeling you're going to tell me," she mumbled.

The teenagers ripped off their jackets. The gold Net Zero logo was splashed across the front of their white T-shirts. "Net Zero is the leading American internet company because they're too legit, too legit to quit, too legit, too legit to quit!" Executing dance moves that would make MC Hammer proud, the trio chanted the chorus of one of the most popular hip-hop songs of all time. And when they ended the routine by executing the splits, Niveah cheered. Other diners applauded, too. Still singing, the teens danced through the dining area and out of sight.

"What do you think?

Niveah spun around on her chair. Damien. In five seconds flat she took in his appearance, noting his chocolate-brown suit and polished shoes. His smile pulled her in, and it took a moment for her to gather her wits. "They were amazing! Where did you find them?"

"They were featured on the local news a few weeks ago and I tracked them down," he explained, taking the seat beside her. "I think they'll be perfect for the Net Zero ad campaign. I haven't finished the spot yet, but I figured if they could make you laugh, they'll be a hit."

"Great work, Damien. Your client is going to be thrilled with what you've come up with."

"Did you have any trouble finding the place? I made a left on Eighth, instead of on Arlington, and ended up driving around in circles for almost ten minutes."

"No, but I almost didn't make it tonight. I was at the office this afternoon, and lost track of time. If the cleaners hadn't interrupted me, I'd still be sitting at my desk organizing the Power Point for the Discreet Boutique ad."

"I've worked with a lot of overachievers in my career, but your commitment to the job puts them all to shame."

Knowing what was coming next, Niveah swiftly changed the subject. "Where did you take Mrs. Garrett-Reed today?"

"She wasn't feeling good, and asked me to take her straight to the hotel. As far as I know, she spent the rest of the day relaxing in her suite."

"Good evening. My name is Stephanos, and I will be your server tonight," the slim, curly haired waiter said. "Can I start you off with something from the bar?"

"I don't drink alcohol when I'm conducting business, so I'll just have a glass of—"

"One cocktail isn't going to kill you." He winked at her, then addressed the waiter. "The lady will have an Aphrodite martini and I'll have a cognac."

"Might you be interested in an appetizer?"

Damien nodded. "We'll have the Mediterranean platter with extra hummus."

The waiter promised to return shortly, and hustled off to the kitchen.

"I wonder where Mr. Russo and Mrs. Garrett are." Niveah glanced at the crowded waiting area. "They should have been here by now."

"I told them our reservations were for seven, so they won't be here for another hour."

Niveah frowned. "Why did you do that?"

"Because I wanted us to talk, *alone*." He rested his forearms on the table. "I thought we could discuss our vision for the creative department. We have very different working styles, but I think it's important that we're on the same page. Things got a bit out of hand at last night's brainstorming session, and I could tell you weren't pleased."

Damien eased forward in his chair. Got so close, Niveah feared he could see the hideous freckles on her cheeks that she'd covered with blush.

"You've got one hell of a team, Niveah. They're far from lazy, and if I had employees like you have here back in New York, I would have been promoted a long time ago."

His words triggered a memory of them laying in bed, eating pizza and discussing her job.

"You must have a very stressful position."

"It's not my job that's going to be the death of me. It's my lazy, dimwitted employees!"

Fear filled her. Had Damien told the team what she said? "Did you tell—"

"I didn't have to. Everyone knows how you feel. Berating people doesn't breed loyalty, and if you don't ease up you'll have no one left working for you. Loosen the reins a bit and you'll see your employees shine."

Incensed by his superior, know-it-all attitude, Niveah glared at him. Damien had no business dolling out advice, and she resented him telling her how to lead her team. But before she could put the arrogant hotshot in his place, the waiter returned.

"Sorry for the delay. We're short-staffed in the kitchen tonight." Bending his knees, he lowered his tray on the table and set down the drinks and appetizers. "Enjoy!"

Niveah waited until the waiter left before speaking her

mind. "I know how to motivate my team, Damien, not you. And I'd appreciate if you kept your opinions to yourself. The last thing I want is dissension growing in the department."

"It's too late. It already has. And unless you change, things are only going to get worse." He looked her straight in the eyes. "Do you know what your nickname is at the office?"

"No," she lied, "and I don't care."

"Everyone calls you the 'Heart of Darkness' because they don't know the real you. You've never given your team the opportunity to see what you're all about."

Now he had her full attention.

"Not only are you sexy as hell, you're smart, insightful and real forward thinking. Your nickname should be 'Lady Day and Night', because there's a lot more to you than meets the eye. Maybe *that's* why I find you so damn appealing."

The softness of his voice gave Niveah pause. And his touching the curve of her elbow prickled her skin. Lust filled her, then desire hit. Her emotions were a swinging pendulum, ranging from one confused emotion to the next.

Damien didn't utter another word. Just looked and stared, making her feel like a science specimen being dissected under a high-powered microscope. He placed a hand on hers, slowly dragging his fingers along her wrist.

In spite of her outward show of calm, her entire body was shaking uncontrollably.

"It's hard for me to refrain from touching you."

Unable to speak, Niveah reached for her glass and drank a mouthful. The gin in the cocktail relaxed her. Loosened her up. Made her feel at ease. Damien was out-and-out flirting with her and she was secretly enjoying every minute of it. Who wouldn't?

"Niveah, I plan to get to know you better inside the boardroom *and* the bedroom."

Shocked by his admission, she sat in perfect silence, unsure of what to say.

"I want another night to please you."

She grunted in response. "I'm surprised to hear you say that, considering how unsatisfied you were on New Year's Eve. According to you, I ranked as one of the worst lovers you've ever had. Then you had the gall to accuse me of stealing your watch."

Niveah saw the fleeting expression of regret that crossed his face. Then humor brightened his eyes and a grin slid across his lips. Wishing she'd kept her mouth shut, she decided to squash any hopes he had of them making love again. "We're colleagues, Damien, and we'll never be anything more. So let's focus on doing our jobs and nailing this Discreet Boutique campaign."

Eager to move on, Niveah picked up her utensils and began eating. The garlic-flavored chicken was delicious, and one piece wasn't enough. Noticing Damien watching her, made her stop. "Don't tell me. I have garlic sauce all over my mouth, right?"

"No, I just enjoy watching you eat. It takes me back to New Year's Eve. To when you—"

"We agreed not to go there, remember?"

"You know, if this advertising thing doesn't work out you could always consider a career in competitive eating. I'd bet on you every time!"

They both laughed.

"I'm a good ol' southern girl, and where I come from food is very important. From the time I could remember, I loved being in the kitchen and inventing new recipes," she explained. "People are always amazed at how much I eat, but I just have a healthy appetite."

"And that's true of the bedroom, too…"

Niveah lifted her eyes from her plate and wished she hadn't. His gaze was searing, and moved over her with deliberate slowness. She'd bet he was still reliving their one-night stand in his mind, and because of his audacious comment, she was, too. To regain focus, she stared down at her hands. Something had to be done about their attraction before she got herself in trouble, but what? Now *that* was the million-dollar question.

"Valentine's Day is coming up. What are your plans?"

The memory of last year's disastrous evening came to mind. Her ex had sat her down, told her they were over and requested the key to his house. "We're all wrong for each other," he'd announced, as if they were discussing something as mundane as the day's weather. "I'm tired of playing second fiddle to your career. I want to be with someone who doesn't blow me off for work, someone who excites me, someone who isn't afraid to let loose in bed. And I've finally found that in *Francesca*." A look of pity showed on his face when he reached over and patted her leg. "I hope there are no hard feelings."

In an effort to distance herself from the past, Niveah considered all of the great things she had going for her. Since the split, she'd gotten a raise, bought a luxury car and paid for repairs to be done on her parents' home. She hadn't been on a single date in the last year, but that didn't mean she wasn't sexy or desirable, right?

Niveah concealed a frown as despair flowed through her. *Who am I fooling?* Being single on Valentine's Day sucked. All of her friends would be off somewhere being wined and dined, and she'd be at home—alone—watching reality TV. *It doesn't get more pathetic than that,* she thought, releasing a deep sigh.

"I might take one of the teenage girls I mentor to the movies," she said, remembering her brief conversation with the high school freshman earlier in the week. "If that falls through, I'll order in a nice dinner and relax at home."

"Want some company?"

"No, thanks." Realizing her words sounded harsh, she

hastened to add, "After spending the entire week surrounded by dozens of people, I look forward to being alone."

"You know what's crazy? We've been working together for weeks, but I still don't know any more about you than I did the night we met."

"There isn't much to tell. I graduated from university, did several stints at various ad agencies before getting hired at Access Media and Entertainment, and for the last ten years—" Niveah broke off when she saw Damien frown. "Why are you staring at me like that?"

"I don't want to know about Niveah Evans, the dynamic creative director, I want to know about Niveah Evans, the woman. Tell me what do you like doing, besides eating pizza in bed and listening to Robin Thicke."

A heady, euphoric feeling fell over Niveah when his moist, oh-so-scrumptious lips parted into a smile. *What's the matter with you?* the voice inside her head asked. Why do you keep making googly eyes at him? Niveah wished she had the answer. Damien wasn't the only attractive man she worked with, but he was the only one she felt flustered around. When it came to dating her colleagues, she'd always had a will of steel. Or at least she used to. Now, she had to draw on every ounce of her self-control every time Damien was within touching distance. What was it about him that made her lose her God-given sense?

"It's not a skill testing question, so quit stalling and tell me what something about you that no one else knows," he said, wiggling his eyebrows.

Realization dawned. That was it! It was his unflappable good humor that made him stand out. He was the type of guy she'd always admired from afar, the type of guy men envied, women admired and children loved.

On the other side of the room, Niveah spotted their waiter, and he wasn't alone. "This discussion is going to have to wait," she told him. "Our esteemed dinner guests are here."

Damien stood, helped Niveah to her feet and rested a hand on the small of her back. "Once this account is in the bag, we'll have plenty of time to get to know each other. I promise."

The Acropolis Greek tavern specialized in fine cuisine, but, since Niveah was full from eating a whole plate of appetizers, she ordered a salmon salad. Like most business dinners, the discussion at the table centered on Wall Street. Niveah was glad that Mr. Russo did most of the talking. That gave her time to regroup. Her conversation with Damien was on her mind, which made it hard to focus on anything else.

"You've been awfully quiet tonight, Niveah. Is everything okay?"

Niveah smiled at Mrs. Garrett-Reed. It was hard to believe that a woman with such striking good looks sat behind a desk all day instead of modeling designer clothes. Her flawless skin, much like her bold haircut and sultry makeup was eye-catching. "I enjoy listening to the different perspectives everyone has on improving the economy," she explained, hoping her excuse was convincing. "I don't know what the answer is, but I'm fascinated by the discussion."

"Mr. Russo tells me that you've been working hard on the menswear campaign. I'd love to hear what you have so far."

"Right now?"

Mrs. Garrett-Reed put down her fork. "As I explained to your boss on the drive over here, my husband and I are taking our daughters to Disneyland next month, and I won't be able to attend the final presentation. Three of my representatives will be here, but I want to be the first one to hear what you've created. That isn't going to be a problem is it?"

Damien spoke up. "Of course not."

"Excellent. So, tell me what your vision is for our new menswear line."

"First, let me begin by saying how honored I am to be

working with you. I read the feature *Business Weekly* did on you three years ago, and I was impressed by your story."

Niveah smiled, but she was gagging on the inside. In the three weeks since Damien had joined the company, she'd seen him finesse, charm and seduce women of all ages, and the smile on Mrs. Garrett-Reed's lips suggested she was enjoying the flattery.

"Is it true you sold lingerie in your dorm room back in university?" Damien asked.

"It sure is!" she said with a soft laugh. "And by the time graduation rolled around, my roommate and I had enough money saved to rent our first boutique."

To demonstrate her interest in the topic, Niveah stopped sneaking looks at Damien and inclined her body toward her client. The VP position was at stake, and so was her reputation as an inventive creative director.

"What made you decide to develop a men's clothing line? You have an enormous female customer base, and your company is growing in leaps and bounds, so why take on such an enormous undertaking now?"

Her face came alive. "I'm glad you asked, Damien. Knowing a bit of background is essential for creating the right image for the ad, isn't it?" Mrs. Garrett-Reed eased forward in her chair. "The line was inspired by my husband. Xavier was always complaining that he couldn't find attractive lounge wear in his size, so I decided to do something about it!"

Niveah finished eating the last of her salad. "Are you eyeing other states besides Minnesota and Florida to carry the line?"

"Definitely. Our goal is to start in a few of the smaller markets, then go worldwide. This is our way of testing the market," she explained. "To create some buzz, we'll launch the menswear brand online in June, which coincides with the opening of our store here in Tampa."

"I think the slogan for the line should be simple,

memorable—something that will appeal to the everyday man. It's also important that the line have its own identity, something that will separate it entirely from Discreet Boutiques. What do you think of the name, S.W.A.G. Fashions?"

Niveah had to admit, she liked the name. She could see it splashed across billboards, on the side of buses, or in the sports section of the local newspaper. "I think you're on to something. The name sounds cool and trendy. Like a magazine."

"Thanks. That's what I was hoping."

Their eyes held for a beat too long. So long, in fact, that Niveah forgot where she was and what they were talking about. The sound of his voice forced her to return to the present.

"I'll have to run the idea by the rest of the team, but I have a feeling they'll love it, too." Mrs. Garrett-Reed had dozens of questions. "What does the ad campaign look like? How much is it going to cost? Will we be on budget?"

Niveah stuck an olive in her mouth. Chewing slowly gave her time to process her options. Should she share the idea she had come up with that afternoon, or keep quiet? Never one to shy away from speaking her mind, she cleared her throat and ignored the puzzled expression on Damien's face. "I know a surefire way to reach consumers," she announced with supreme confidence. "Research shows that women buy clothes, toiletries and fragrances for their husbands, friends and significant others, so I developed a campaign with the female consumer in mind. The slogan is—'S.W.A.G. Fashions, where sensuality meets masculinity'."

Mrs. Garrett-Reed pumped a fist in the air, as if she was cheering on her favorite sporting team. "That's an awesome slogan! One our target audience is sure to respond to!"

On the surface, Niveah was as calm as an emergency room nurse, but inside she was brimming with pride. It felt great having her client's approval, and when Damien raised his glass to her in salute, she couldn't stop herself from smiling. "I think we should kick off the line by doing something completely out of the box."

Mrs. Garrett-Reed didn't speak, but Niveah could tell by the way she nodded that she was impressed. Encouraged, Niveah went on, sharing her thoughts and ideas as they came to her. When she finished her spiel, everyone around the table was smiling.

"I *love* the idea of the twelve-month calendar, and you're right, getting celebrities to pose in the merchandise will shoot our first-quarter profits straight through the roof." Her eyes shone with excitement and she could hardly sit still in her chair. "This will only work if we use the right people. Who do you have in mind to capture the spread?"

"Kenyon Blake is my top choice for lead photographer. He's one of the best in the business, and comes highly recommended."

Mrs. Garrett-Reed nodded her head vigorously, her long bangs sweeping across her forehead. "I saw his spread in *Rolling Stone* a few months ago. I loved the pictures he took of the White House female staff decked out in black leather. Can we afford him?"

"Kenyon's on assignment right now in Cuba," she explained, "but his agent promised to get back to me next week."

"Have you selected the models yet?"

"No. I wanted to run my ideas by you first."

"I might be able to help in that department." Damien proceeded to tell them about some of the celebrity contacts he'd made over the course of his twelve-year career. "Heavyweight boxer Rashawn 'The Glove' Bishop and former NFL running back Terrence Franklin have become good friends of mine, and if we agree to make a donation to their favorite charities, they'll probably do the ads pro bono—providing they have time in their schedules."

"Really?" Niveah raised her eyebrows. "It's hard to believe

that two big-name athletes would be so generous, especially when all of the other celebrities I've contacted are charging a thousand dollars an hour. Are you sure about this, Damien? I don't mean to be pessimistic, but that sounds too good to be true."

"I did a commercial last year to raise awareness of Huntington's disease, and they both lent their support to the project. Their involvement did wonders for the organization."

Niveah's skepticism turned to awe. Up until then, she'd pegged Damien as a player of the worst kind, a man who lived for babes, beer and sports cars, but hearing about his involvement in such a worthwhile cause left her speechless.

"I fly out tomorrow morning, but I'd love to have a written proposal to take back to Minneapolis with me."

There was no way Niveah could pull everything together in twelve hours, but when she saw Mr. Russo's eyebrows crawl up his receding hairline, she quickly agreed to the request. If she wanted that VP position, she'd better get the job done and fast.

"If you'll excuse me, I have to go powder my nose." Mrs. Garrett-Reed slid her legs out from under the table. "Ms. Evans, why don't you join me?"

Niveah grabbed her purse, and followed the statuesque entrepreneur back through the restaurant. Couples sat along the bar, sipping wine, nibbling on cheese and grooving to the music playing. The ballad stirred something within her, and like a hundred times that week, her thoughts turned to Damien and the night they'd spent together. Niveah was so busy reminiscing, she almost tripped when Mrs. Garrett-Reed stopped abruptly.

"Please sit down. There's something I'd like to discuss with you."

The bartender hustled over as the women slid onto the metal bar stools.

"What can I get for you two lovely ladies?"

"We'll both have a glass of sangria."

"I'm thrilled to be working with you, Mrs. Garrett-Reed," Niveah said, hoping to alleviate the tension she felt in the air, "and I'm going to make this ad campaign a hit."

"I just hope your feelings for Damien don't interfere with your ability to do your job."

Shock paralyzed Niveah. Struck dumb, she stared at Mrs. Garrett-Reed in amazement.

"Don't deny that you're attracted to him, Ms. Evans, because it's as clear as day. In fact, watching the two of you during dinner reminded me of the first time I met my husband." A wistful smile, one that caused her eyes to glaze over with happiness, filled her lips. "He couldn't stand me, but after our first kiss, I knew he was the only man for me."

"There is nothing going on between Mr. Hunter and me." Her voice sped up, and beads of sweat broke out on her forehead. "To be honest, I can't stand him."

"There's no reason to lie, Niveah. And just so we're clear, I don't have a problem with you two dating, or doing whatever it is you're doing. I firmly believe that a woman can have it all. Love, family *and* a successful career. It takes some juggling, but it can definitely be done."

"Mrs. Garrett-Reed, I assure you I am fully committed to this campaign."

"Good, that's just what I wanted hear. I'm not trying to discourage you from seeing Damien, I just don't want anything to get in the way of you doing your job. I've heard great things about you, and I love what I've seen so far."

"Thank you. I take my job seriously, and I have the track record to prove it."

"Oh, there's just one more thing," she said, holding up her index finger. "When you and Damien quit playing these mind games, and hook up once and for all, I want an invitation to the wedding. Actually, I'll need four. My twin girls just *love* weddings."

"Nothing is going on. We're professionals, and we act as such at all times."

Mrs. Garrett-Reed smirked. "Who are you trying to convince, Niveah, me or you?"

Chapter 8

The driver of the silver Cadillac slammed on his breaks, and Damien swerved to avoid hitting him. By the time the left lane cleared and he inched around the old hooptie, the light turned red. Damien tossed the elderly driver a murderous look, but instantly felt guilty. It wasn't the old man's fault he was miserable. He'd had a productive afternoon, finalizing the details of the Net Zero ad campaign, but he still felt depressed. And Niveah Evans was to blame.

A car horn blared. Damien stepped on the gas, and his red Mitsubishi Eclipse shot through the intersection. As he cruised down the street, he found himself thinking about the creative director with the sultry smile. How was he supposed to seduce her when she was avoiding him? Not seeing her was killing him. If she wasn't out of the office, she was tied up in meetings or having lunch with her girlfriends, or...the list was endless. Damien was frustrated by her lack of availability. He didn't want to force himself on her, but what other choice did he have? It was either wait around for her to come to her senses, or step up his game, because a woman like Niveah wouldn't be on the market much longer.

Damien felt as if his head was going to explode. It wasn't normal to think about a woman every second of every day, was it? It had been weeks since they'd made love, but he still couldn't move past it. The memory of Niveah perched on his lap, riding him into oblivion, was forever stamped in his mind. They'd been intimate three times that night, but it hadn't been enough, and he suspected that when it came to Niveah his appetite for her would never be filled.

Turning up the radio didn't drown out his thoughts. The stress of the last three weeks was getting to him, and when he'd glimpsed Niveah this afternoon in the staff room, she'd looked exhausted. A few nights of carnal pleasure was exactly what they needed to revitalize them, so why was she fighting it? He'd never had to seduce a woman before, but if being more aggressive would help him get Niveah back in his bed, then he was all for it. All he had to figure out now was when to launch his attack.

A grin stretched across his mouth. A trip to her office after dark was definitely in order. Niveah was a happy but busy type who didn't need a man, but enjoyed sex. *Just like me.* They were a perfect fit, completely in sync sexually, and it was up to him to prove it to her.

Damien parked in the Golden Gate plaza and locked his car. Shoppers perused the high-end outlet stores, and couples streamed in and out of the movie theatre. *What am I going to do about this situation with Niveah?* Not having her in his bed was driving him crazy. His body ached for her, and as he passed Discreet Boutiques, he pictured her in the short lace number hanging in the store window. He didn't want to offend Niveah by buying something racy from the boutique, but it couldn't hurt to have a quick look around. He'd call it research. After all, how could he effectively design an ad campaign if he didn't know anything about the product he was selling?

Two saleswomen wearing bright smiles greeted him with a warm hello when he entered the store. As expected, bras, panties and camisoles were displayed on round glass tables. Enormous Valentine's Day sale signs promised twenty-five percent off any item and a free box of chocolates with every purchase.

Perusing the boutique didn't give Damien any ideas of what to buy for Niveah. Unable to decide between a silk robe and a black leather angel costume he couldn't stop picturing her in, he wandered over to one of the shelves at the rear of the store. A box tied with a gargantuan red ribbon caught his eye. A Mile High Tool Kit? Picking up the package, he read the contents listed on the box. He'd never had sex on an airplane and never been tempted to, but then again, he'd never traveled with a woman who looked like Niveah. What could be more thrilling than seeing her bent over a sink, her legs spread wide, moans streaming from her lips—

"Sir, is there something I can help you with?"

Damien glanced over his shoulder. He opened his mouth to decline the clerk's offer, but the words stuck in the back of his throat. As if in a trance, he stood mutely, staring out the front window. His eyes zeroed in on its target: Niveah. She always dressed so prim and proper to work, but this afternoon she looked like the sexy siren he'd bedded on New Year's Eve.

His legs felt rubbery, weak. But seeing a drop-dead-gorgeous woman could bring any man to his knees, and remembering how passionate Niveah was between the sheets made his heart threaten to break out of his chest, one deafening beat at a time. Appraising her outfit gave him great pleasure. Her floral print dress fell softly against her skin, and the open toe sandals elongated her legs. Free of that tight, hideous bun, her curly brown hair blew every which way.

His eyes followed her from the parking lot to the movie theater. Damn, she was something. Not just smart, but creative and independent, too. And then there was that sexy little body of hers. Damien liked the whole package—the lush lips, that firm butt, the way she moved through space. He felt a rising need in his groin, and snapped out of his daze.

Dropping the Mile High Tool Kit on the shelf, Damien strode purposely out of the boutique, determined to connect with the woman he couldn't seem to get out of his mind.

"Has Jamaal tried to kiss you?"

Niveah saw the twinkle in Shavone Andrews's eyes and knew the answer to her question. The fifteen-year-old girl was one of the three teenagers Niveah mentored, and by far the most grown-up. Street smart and wise beyond her years, Niveah feared the high school freshman would be taken advantage of by some cute older guy and end up another teenage statistic.

Since Mr. Andrews was working, she'd agreed to chaperone Shavone's first date with Jamaal Phillips. The honor roll student was a bright kid with great manners, but he was still a boy—a pubescent boy who looked twice his age—and Niveah didn't trust him. "I hope that's all you've done," she warned, adding a note of severity to her tone. "I know you think you're grown, Shavone, but when it comes to the opposite sex you have a lot to learn."

"Ms. Niveah, we're not doing it or anything. We just kiss and…and stuff."

"What kind of stuff?" Niveah could feel her blood pressure rise, but spoke in a calm, soothing voice that masked her anger. "It's okay to like boys, Shavone, but don't do anything to disappoint your dad. You mean the world to him."

"You're not going to sit with us are you?"

"Of course I am. I have to ensure that Jamaal doesn't get any ideas," she explained, speaking loud enough for the young man to hear. "You wouldn't believe what some kids do in the movie theater when they think no one's looking."

"We're not going to do anything. I promise."

"I told your father I'd look out for you, and I can't do that from across the room."

Her lips puckered into a scowl. "I asked you to come with us because I thought you'd be cool," she grumbled. "If I had known you were going to trip, I would have just snuck out."

"All right, I won't sit beside you, but remember what I told you back at the youth center."

"'Good girls don't let boys put their hands up their skirts,'" she recited, rolling her eyes. "How can I forget? You write it on my Facebook page every day."

While the teens talked about basketball tryouts at their school, Niveah checked her cell phone for missed calls. The first message was from her parents. Calling them back was out of the question. All her mom wanted to talk about these days was visiting Tampa, and with everything Niveah had going on at work, she didn't have time to play tour guide.

The next three messages were from Damien, and each one was funnier than the last. Hearing his voice excited her, and she couldn't resist smiling. The New Yorker was unlike anyone she'd ever met. He was a student of the world, a man who loved hip-hop, extreme sports and traveling the globe. Being around Damien invigorated her, made her feel like she was back in high school, discovering boys for the first time. And God help her the next time he touched her. She'd barely been able to contain herself the last time. If her boss and Mrs. Garrett-Reed hadn't showed up at the Acropolis Greek tavern when they did, she probably would have ended up kissing him right there at their intimate corner table.

"What are you doing in my neck of the woods?"

Niveah glanced up from her cell phone and drew a sharp breath. Her inner voice told her to run—and run fast—but she ignored the message. The truth was, the combined effects of Damien's cologne and his easy grin rendered her speechless. As Niveah checked him out, she wondered if there was any truth to what he'd said. This theater *was* the one he had mentioned to her last week. Had she subconsciously come here in the hopes of running into him?

"I wish you dressed like this during business hours. You look incredible."

"Thanks, so do you." And did he ever. Blue was definitely his color, and she loved how he'd paired his casual sports coat with jeans and Timberland boots. He was positively dreamy, and seized the attention of several women standing near the concession stand. "I'm sorry I missed your call earlier," Niveah said, gathering her wits. "I had a meeting with Kenyon Blake this afternoon, and when I got back to the office, there seemed to be one problem after another. Needless to say, it's been one of those days."

Niveah heard Shavone giggle and remembered she wasn't alone. She introduced the teens to Damien, and raised an eyebrow when Jamaal shook his hand.

"Do you guys mind if I join you?"

"That would be great!" Shavone nodded emphatically. "Jamaal and I are sitting *alone,* but you're more than welcome to keep Ms. Niveah company."

"Welcome to Paramount Theaters." From behind the desk, the clerk waved them over. He punched in the necessary information for the movie they wanted to see, then said, "Your total is fifty-two dollars and eighty cents."

"I've got it." Damien stepped forward, and paid the cashier.

"Thanks. That's very kind of you." Niveah watched the teens wander over to the arcade. Concerned about the hand Jamaal had resting on Shavone's butt, she moved swiftly toward the pair. They were only a few feet away, but Niveah wanted the honor roll student to know she was hip to his game.

"You gave me back too much change."

Niveah stopped. Was Damien actually correcting the cashier's mistake? She turned around and watched as he handed the young man back several dollar bills. *That's not something you see every day.* Her ex would have taken the money and headed to the nearest strip club.

"Ms. Niveah, can we get some junk food?"

While they waited for their order, Damien asked the kids about school. Niveah listened, impressed with the advice he gave, and how naturally he interacted with the teens. And when they entered the theater, he suggested they give the kids some space. "The back row is empty," he said, gesturing to the vacant seats, "and you can still spy on Shavone and Jamaal from here."

Theater 8 was saturated with the scent of buttered popcorn. Intimately aware of Damien beside her, Niveah watched him out of the corner of her eye. *This man is simply gorgeous,* she thought, itching to touch him. "Something's obviously on your mind," she said, offering a smile. "Do you want to talk about it?"

"Sure, why not." Damien propped his elbow on the armrest and inclined his body toward hers. "I'm interested in someone. A real smart, dynamic lady. But she won't give me the time of day. Every time I step to her, she blows me off. What do you think I should do?"

For a second she thought he might be referring to one of their colleagues, but when he winked at her, Niveah knew she was the woman in question. Her entire body throbbed with excitement. Snippets of her conversation with Ms. Garrett-Reed came to mind. Hadn't she assured the entrepreneur that nothing was going on between her and Damien? "Maybe she doesn't know you're interested. Ask her out again, and see what she says."

"What are you doing after this?"

"Nothing, once I drop the kids off, I'm free."

"Great. We can go to Blue Shark. They have the best blues band in the city."

Niveah coiled a curl around her index finger. It felt good

being with Damien, and having his undivided attention. Roxi was right. Flirting with a fine, handsome man *did* make her feel alive. "For someone who just landed a six-figure Nike account, you sure have a lot of free time on your hands."

"The account's in the bag, so that leaves me with plenty of time to romance you."

A hush fell over the audience when the lights dimmed. Leaning back comfortably in her seat, she allowed herself to relax. It was the end of another long day, and watching a romantic comedy was a surefire way to relieve stress.

Fifteen minutes later, Niveah thought about taking out her hand held and checking her email. The movie was so boring, she was starting to doze off.

"Isn't Tracy Morgan hilarious?"

Niveah managed a weak smile. Instead of staring up at the screen, she peered down the aisle. Jamaal had his arm around Shavone's shoulders and his lips against her ear. The light from the screen illuminated the smile on the teen's rosy lips. To find out where the kid was resting his *other* hand, Niveah eased forward in her seat.

"They're fine," Damien told her. "Concentrate on the movie. This is the best part."

"You're actually enjoying this?"

"No. If it were up to me, we'd be back at your place."

"Doing what?" Captivated by the sudden huskiness of his voice, she inched closer, desperate to hear more. The kiss surprised her. Not the fact that he'd done it, but just how good it felt when his lips touched hers. Niveah wanted this, wanted to be touched and caressed by him.

I have to draw the line before things get out of hand, she thought. *One more kiss and then I'll stop.* Inclining her head sideways, she locked her arms tightly around his neck. Making out in the back row of a movie theatre was juvenile and—Niveah tossed her head back—oh such fun. He felt like heaven, tasted like heaven, and he touched her just the way she liked.

Pleasure welled up inside her. Niveah loved how Damien's lips and hands moved simultaneously, as if to an indiscernible rhythm. A curse ripped from his mouth when she brushed her fingers over his erection. Damien always played by the rules, always did the right thing, and seeing him lose control was a huge turn-on. Wanting more, she slid a hand under his shirt, and stroked his chest.

Niveah couldn't believe what she was doing, but she didn't stop. His kiss quenched a deep-seated thirst, and made it impossible to do anything but feel. Grabbing the back of his head, she pressed her body hard against his. Damien's lips were like nothing else, and Niveah was desperate for more. His hands were instruments of pleasure—caressing her cheeks, rubbing her shoulders, stroking her hair. Having her breasts fondled had never brought her to climax before, but when Damien tweaked her nipples, it felt like a volcano had erupted between her thighs.

Mustering all of her strength, she pulled out of Damien's arms. Shame and guilt churned in her stomach. A fine role model she was. Preaching morality one minute, and making out with Damien at the back of the movie theater the next. What would she have said if someone had caught them? She wanted to cultivate pride and self-respect in the teens she mentored, and fooling around with Damien was definitely sending the wrong message.

Niveah stopped beating herself up. Kissing wasn't all that bad, was it? It's not like Damien had ripped off her clothes, and bent her over the seat—

Yeah, but you wanted him to.

The idea couldn't be any truer. For the second time in weeks, she'd fallen victim to Damien's husky voice and those to-die-for kisses. His smile had the power to quiet her fears, and his touch easily silenced that niggling voice at the back of her head. Despite all that was at stake, Niveah wanted to make love to Damien again, and the realization stunned her. Why couldn't she shake her attraction to him? And why did it seem as if this thing between them was suddenly bigger than the both of them?

"I know somewhere we can go." His eyes were alight with anticipation, and as they slid down his body, his hands reached out and teased. "You leave first and I'll follow you."

There's only so much a girl can take, Niveah thought, loving how his fingers played gently over her thighs. Having sex in public had always been her secret fantasy, but tonight wasn't the night, and Paramount Theaters wasn't the place. "I'm supposed to be chaperoning Shavone's date. Not making out with you."

"You're right. I lost control. I'm sorry."

His silky falsetto made Niveah all but forget her name.

"I'm going to get out of here before we get arrested for indecent exposure."

"Okay. I guess I'll see you on Monday then."

"Niveah, this is far from over," he vowed. His appraising glance was too much for her, so Niveah stared ahead at the screen. Images swam before her. *What movie is this again?*

"I'll meet you back at your place in an hour."

"But you don't know where I live."

Damien wore his most innocent face. "I know a lot more than you think I do." He was massaging her thighs now, causing ripples of pleasure to career through her core.

"I thought you wanted to go to Blue Shark to listen to some live music."

"It's the most romantic day of the year, and I want to spend it alone with you. We'll just have coffee and talk. No pressure, okay?"

Niveah knew his suggestion had nothing to do with a cup of Folger's and everything to do with them making love. Fear and excitement churned in her stomach. Stamping out the desire pulsing through her horny body wasn't easy, but necessary. Damien was one of those party-hopping, always looking for some booty type brothers, and the minute she forgot that, she was toast. "I wasn't born yesterday, Damien. I know where this is headed, and I'm not interested."

"I'm well aware of the pitfalls that come with hooking up with a colleague, but I'm willing to take that risk."

"But I'm not." It had been lust-at-first sight for the both of them, and with each stolen kiss, the fire blazed hotter, but that didn't mean that Niveah was willing to throw caution to the wind and indulge in a reckless affair.

"Let's stop creeping around the issue and cut straight to the point." There was a hitch in his tone, a dangerously sexy note that was heavy with sensuality. "I want you in my bed and I know that's where you want to be, so why don't you make it easy on yourself and stop fighting it, because I'm not going to give up until I have you again." Then he stole a kiss, got up, and strolled out of the theater as if the matter was closed.

Chapter 9

"What's this nonsense about you not wanting us to come visit?"

The headache that had started when Niveah left the movie theater pulsed behind her right eye. Head shots of two dozen male models covered the kitchen island, but as she listened to her father reprimand her for being insensitive to her mother's feelings, she lost interest in selecting the remaining models for next Friday's S.W.A.G. photo shoot.

"Dad, of course I want to see you. It's just that now isn't the best time."

"According to you, it's never a good time," he countered. "I'm beginning to think you're hiding something, Norma-Jean. Are you pregnant?"

Niveah burst out laughing. "No, and I'm not hiding a secret love child, either."

"Then what is it? You're the only daughter we have, and not seeing you is killing us."

Her shoulders sagged under the weight of her father's

words. He rarely discussed his feelings, and although she suspected he'd been coached by her mother, knowing that she'd hurt him made her feel terrible. "When do you want to come?"

"The last week in April. We were planning on booking our tickets on Wednesday. Greyhound has a two-for-one seat sale that we can't afford to miss."

"I don't want you guys taking the bus here," she told him, slowly warming to the idea of a one-week visit. "I'll book two first class tickets on American Airlines tomorrow, *and* six nights at The Ritz-Carlton. How does that sound? Think you'll like staying in a fancy, five-star suite with all the comforts of home?"

"A hotel!"

"Mom?" Niveah stared down at the receiver. "I didn't know you were on the line. Why didn't you say anything?"

"Because you and your father were having a private conversation, and I didn't want to butt in. Now what's this prattle about us staying at some out-of-the-way hotel?"

Reaching for a handful of pretzels in the ceramic bowl, Niveah wondered if it was too late to order a pizza. She was hungry, and this salty, low-fat snack wasn't cutting it. "I just thought you and Dad would like having your own space."

"But you live in a huge house! I don't want to hear another word about us staying somewhere else. If we can't stay with you, then we won't come at all."

Promise? Niveah thought, but didn't say. This was another reason why she was reluctant to have her parents visit. Her dad was easy going, content to lie on the couch and watch college football, while her mom lived to fuss. Their seven-day trip to Puerto Rico five years ago had been a disaster. Her mother had complained about the cost of the amenities at the resort, fretted every time a panhandler approached her and refused to eat the local food.

"So it's settled," her mom said, "we're coming to Tampa and we're staying with you."

Niveah didn't have the energy to argue. "I'm sorry I suggested the hotel in the first place. I didn't mean to offend you, Mom, I just want you to be comfortable while you're here."

"As long as we're together we'll be fine, Norma-Jean."

The doorbell rang and Niveah cranked her neck toward the foyer. *I know that's not Damien,* she thought, nervously biting the side of her lip. He had no business showing up at her house unannounced, especially after she'd told him to stay away.

"Who's at your door at this time of night?" her parents asked in unison.

"I have no idea."

Mr. Evans sounded worried. "You better be careful, honey. It could be some deranged drug addict looking for money."

Niveah moved the phone away from her mouth so her father wouldn't hear her laugh. He loved watching *Cops,* and every other sentence out of his mouth was about ruthless drug dealers corrupting big cities. *As if drug use isn't a problem in Chickasaw. It was when I was a teenager, and I bet it's even worse now.* But Niveah didn't tell her dad that. He'd been raised on a five-acre farm in Mobile County, and hated when people criticized his beloved hometown.

"Use your cell phone to call the cops," Mr. Evans instructed. "We'll hold the line."

"It's probably just my neighbor coming by to borrow some…sugar."

Her mother scoffed. "At nine forty-six? No one in their right mind would do that."

The harsh knock on the kitchen window startled Niveah.

"What was that? Is someone trying to break in?"

"No, of course not, Dad. I told you it's…the woman next door."

"You're sure everything's okay?"

"Uh-huh." Niveah heard the back door jiggle, and felt a lump of fear in the pit of her stomach. What if it wasn't Damien, but someone high on…

Shaking her head cleared the thought from her mind. This is what she got listening to her paranoid, overprotective father. Just because she lived within walking distance of a youth shelter didn't mean her life was in danger. "I'll call you guys tomorrow."

"Call us back if you need anything. Anything at all."

Niveah almost laughed. As if her father could do anything from five hundred miles away. "I will. Bye." She clicked off the phone and dropped it on the table. Maybe if she sat perfectly still the caller would go away. No such luck. The doorbell chimed again. Then the person knocked *and* rang at the same time. When her cell phone buzzed, and Damien's name popped up on the screen, Niveah knew he was the nuisance outside her door. Reluctantly, she rose from her chair and padded across the floor.

In the backyard, Damien bracketed his face with his hands and peered through the kitchen window. The lights were on and he could see the silhouette of a woman sitting at the island. Why wasn't Niveah answering the door? Surely she'd heard him ringing the bell the last ten minutes.

Damien glanced at his watch and was stunned to see how late it was. That's why Niveah wasn't answering the door. She was upset and Damien didn't blame her. Not when he was showing up hours after he'd promised to be there. It didn't matter that he had a good excuse for being late. He'd let her down, and if he wanted to get back on her good side, he'd have to do a whole lot of begging.

How had this night gone so wrong? he wondered, staring

up at the starlit sky. When he left the movie theater, he'd planned to run into the mall to buy Niveah a Valentine's Day gift, but he'd received a call on his cell phone that changed everything. By the time he got gone home, and gotten the situation under control, it was nearly nine o'clock. More than two hours *after* he'd told Niveah he'd be at her house.

Damien knew he had his work cut out for him, and when he called Niveah's cell phone and it went straight to voicemail, he feared he'd blown his chance. Damien told himself he didn't care, told himself that Niveah wasn't worth all this trouble. *Sure, that's why you've been driving around the city searching for the perfect Valentine's Day gift for her.*

The scent rising from the bags of Greek takeout sitting at his feet caused Damien's stomach to grumble. Left with no options, Damien headed in the direction of the picnic table. Since Niveah wouldn't let him inside, he'd just have to lure her outside.

"What do you want?"

Damien spun around. Bright lights flooded the backyard, temporarily blinding him. The storm door was only open a crack, but he could see Niveah leaning against the door frame, a peeved expression on her face. Always perfectly put together, it was a surprise to see her in a white University of Florida T-shirt, cotton shorts and bare feet.

"I'd really appreciate it if you went home." A scowl set firmly in place, she tapped her foot impatiently on the welcome mat. "This is a quiet family neighborhood, and if you don't quit banging on the windows someone's going to call the police."

"I can explain."

"Explain what?" Her cheeks flushed deep red, revealing just how angry she was. "I don't even know why you're here. I told you not to come, remember?"

"I had a family emergency."

Niveah fixed her arms across her chest like a shield of protective armor. "Sure you did. That's why you smell like cheap, bargain-store perfume."

Damien sniffed his shirt. Damn, he did! In his haste to leave the house, he'd forgotten to change, and now this oversight might cost him spending time with her. Back in the day, he would have used every trick in the book to sway her, but Niveah was different than any of the other women he'd hooked up with. She was special, rare, as precious as a vintage bottle of wine. He wasn't looking for a long-term commitment, but he could see himself kicking it with her for a long time. "There was a situation at home that I needed to take care of, and it took longer than I expected." To win her trust, he made it plain. "I wasn't with another woman, Niveah. At least not the way you think. I haven't been with anyone else since we met. I swear."

"What's in the bag?" she asked, her tone losing some of its hostility. "I smell mushrooms."

"I swung by the Acropolis and grabbed us some dinner." He saw the corners of her lips rise in a half smile, and knew that he was making progress. "It's Valentine's Day; I couldn't come by empty-handed."

"It looks like you have a lot more than just food."

"I have movies, popcorn and several boxes of those strawberry shortcake rolls you love so much. I heard you have a secret stash of them in your office, is that true?"

Niveah fought against a smile. She had to hand it to Damien, he was an incredibly observant man. Everyone at Access Media and Entertainment knew of her weakness for fine food, and Damien had showed up on her doorstep with enough appetizers to cater a small dinner party. But this was an intimate party for two, and before Niveah did something she'd later regret, she weighed the pros and cons of inviting him inside.

The strength of his gaze worried her. It was too strong, too intense, and made her reminisce about all the delicious things he done to her on New Year's Eve.

"I'm not here to get you into bed, Niveah. That's not what tonight is about. It's about two colleagues who mutually respect each other sharing a meal."

"I can handle that."

A grin dimpled his cheeks. "Good, so can I come in now? I'm starving!"

Niveah hesitated. If she allowed Damien inside, he'd think that she liked him, but if she didn't he'd leave and take the food with him. Stepping aside, she welcomed him into her home and closed the door behind her when he crossed the threshold.

Inquisitive by nature, Damien glanced around the main floor. An archway separated the kitchen from the living room, but he could see expensive, dark furniture, a two-sided fireplace and potted plants on the other side of the wall. "This is a nice place."

"Thanks." Niveah went over to the cabinet and grabbed plates and cutlery.

"I see you've been busy working," he said, picking up a head shot. "Now I understand why it took you so long to answer the door. You were checking out model profiles."

"Hey, since you're here, you can help me fill the last few spots."

Damien pulled back his sleeve and tapped his watch. "I'm off the clock, and so are you."

"You must spend a lot of money on jewelry, because that watch looks identical to the one you lost on New Year's Eve."

The expression on his face was one of regret. "This is the watch I thought you stole from me. A maid at the hotel found it and turned it in. I'm sorry for accusing you of stealing it."

Niveah couldn't think straight. Her thoughts were twisted, jumbled up like a ball of colored string in a kitten's paw. Her ears had to be plugged, because it sounded like Damien was apologizing for calling her a thief. She couldn't move her lips, couldn't make her mouth form a single word, so she stood there mutely, taking everything in. There was a note of sincerity in his voice, and he looked genuinely sorry. But that didn't mean she believed him. Maybe his heartfelt speech was nothing more than a trick to knock her off her game. That VP position was hers for the taking, and she wouldn't let Damien or anyone else steal it from her. "I accept your apology, but this truce between us isn't going to stop me from landing that promotion."

"That makes two of us." He pulled out her chair. "Now that that's settled, let's get into the grub. The tortellini's getting cold, and I'm hungrier than a *Biggest Loser* contestant!"

They shared a laugh.

Damien dished out the food and opened the wine. "Here's to the best Valentine's Day ever," he announced, clinking his glass against hers. "And to one hell of a raise in June!"

Niveah nodded. "I'll drink to that."

"I called you a few times but you didn't pick up. Were you on the phone with one of those hunky models or just avoiding me?"

"I was talking to my parents."

"Is everything okay?"

Unburdening herself to Damien might come back to haunt her, but she opened up and told him about her guilt-ridden conversation with her parents. "I have mixed feelings about them coming to visit. I want to see them, but I just don't have the time to entertain."

"Then make time," he told her, tasting the olive bread. "You only have one set of parents, and once they're gone, they're gone. Cherish every moment you have with them because you never know what may happen down the road."

"You must have a really good relationship with your parents."

"They mean the world to me."

Niveah scooped rice onto her plate. "Do you have any siblings?"

"Yeah, two sisters. They're married, with a couple kids apiece, and live in Long Island."

"It must be hard being out here alone."

"Not really. I've been coming to Tampa since I was a kid, and it's been great to reconnect with some of the guys I used to hang out with. It's amazing how much everyone's changed in the last fifteen years."

Niveah stopped chewing. "I thought this was your first trip here."

"Nope. I have relatives here, so every summer my mom shipped me off to work at her brother's construction business. I even lived here during my senior year in high school."

"You neglected to mention that when we met."

"Why? Would it have made any difference?"

"Well, no, but…"

"Oh, I get it. You liked the idea of being with a roughneck, a bad boy, someone who grew up on the hood. And discovering that I'm a good ol' boy who also lived in the Sunshine State ruined the fantasy, huh?"

Niveah swallowed a laugh. Damien was teasing her, but she didn't mind. He looked as happy as a king on his throne, and spent the rest of the meal making her laugh. The stories he shared about his college days and pledging every fraternity on campus left her in stitches.

Once the dishwasher was loaded and the leftovers were put in the fridge, they settled into the living room. Dessert was a sweet mousse, flavored with rum, and when Niveah finished her second slice she had the most delicious buzz.

"What movies did you bring?" she asked, peering into the white shopping bag. "I hope you didn't bring anything corny, because after watching that movie today I've had about all the sophomoric humor I can stand."

"I figured as much, so I rented some erotic thrillers. I think we should watch *Forbidden Fruit* first. It's one of my favorites."

Niveah pointed the remote at the flat-screen TV. "I've never heard of it. What's it about?"

"It's about a guy who falls for his friend's wife, and all the problems their affair causes."

"Have you ever been in a situation like that?"

"I might be a lot of things, Niveah, but an asshole isn't one of them."

"I didn't say you were," she began, instantly feeling contrite, "it's just that there's been a lot of talk about you and Essence hanging out after work—"

Damien broke in. "She's going through a rough time in her marriage, and needed someone to talk to. We're friends and nothing more."

"Are you seeing anyone at work, romantically?"

"You mean besides you?"

Niveah ignored the quip. Damien was out-and-out flirting with her, but she was too smart to fall for his tricks. He was unpredictable and determined, and there was no telling what he would do if she took the bait. "Most of the women at the office think you're a player, and—"

"The only opinion that matters to me is yours. So tell me, Niveah, what do you think?"

"I think you're the most spoiled, charismatic man to ever walk the face of the earth, and I want you more than I've ever wanted anyone before."

Niveah cupped a hand over her mouth. How could she have spoken her deepest, darkest, most intimate thought out loud? She saw a flash of desire in Damien's eyes. Then he leaned over and kissed her so passionately she collapsed back onto the cushions. His fingertips grazed her collarbone, shooting pleasurable ripples to her core. Niveah tried to pull away, but he held on tighter. A sensual wave slaughtered her, leaving her feeling physically spent.

Niveah struggled for control, but when Damien cupped her breast and flicked his thumb over her nipple, she gave up the fight. He'd lit a spark in her she'd never known was there. He made her believe in love at first sight, and all the emotions Sade sang about in her songs. That's why she sank into him, locked her arms around his neck and kissed him back.

They were all over each other, teasing, caressing, feasting on each other's lips. Niveah couldn't get enough. Desperate for more, she raked her hands up his back. Damien moaned something fierce and stepped up his game. Slowly, oh so slowly, he slipped his tongue into her mouth. Stars gathered in Niveah's eyes. His kisses, like his hands, were detrimental to her well-being. They were addictive, potent and the best damn thing she had ever tasted.

Damien outlined her ear with his tongue and a dizzying, head-to-toe warmth spread through her. Niveah was on the verge of coming, and she was still fully dressed. His touch was like nothing else, and she welcomed the feel of his hands on her breasts.

"You are so damn sexy."

Sexy? Niveah almost choked on the word. Surely he was joking. She was wearing old clothes, her hair was in a sloppy ponytail and she smelled like garlic. If they were going to make love, she'd have to go freshen up, because she felt anything but sexy.

"I know I promised I wouldn't try anything, but…" Damien

trailed off, as he drew his lips across her cheek, her ear and her neck, "I can't control myself when I'm around you."

I know the feeling. His voice was laced with need, urgency, making Niveah think that he was a slave to his desires, too. Damien took off her shorts and underwear, then spread her legs wide open. The words *amazing, exquisite* and *divine* streamed from her lips when he dipped his tongue into her treasure.

Flat on her back, her legs positioned over his shoulders, she gripped his head to keep his mouth in place. His lips felt crazy good, better than she'd ever dreamed. Like a thirsty man who'd stumbled upon a brook while wandering in the desert, he eagerly drank from her oasis, swirling and lapping his tongue inside her walls. Niveah felt as if she was outside of her body, thousands of miles away. And when Damien ran his hands up over her curves, she moaned her pleasure.

"Where's your bedroom?"

"I-I-I don't know..." she said, gasping for breath. His tongue stimulated her orgasm and her arms and legs quivered. Overtaken by the spasms that raked her body, she pitched her head back, closed her eyes, and dug her fingernails into his shoulders.

"Ah, hell, forget the bedroom." Damien discarded his clothes in record speed. Rejoining her on the couch, he slid on the condom he retrieved from his wallet, and settled between her legs. "I can't wait to be inside you," he whispered. "I've wanted this for weeks."

"Give me a minute. I need a moment to catch my breath."

"Oh no you don't."

Damien kissed her. It was soft, sweet and tinged with passion. Working her way up his back, she massaged from his shoulders to his neck, hoping to convey how desperately she wanted him, too. And once she took a quick shower and changed into some nice lingerie, she'd be ready to put it on him. "I'll be right back."

"I'm not letting you out of my sight."

Niveah giggled when he pinned her arms down. "I knew you were trouble the moment we met. Instead of approaching you at the bar, I should have run in the opposite direction!"

"But you didn't. You followed me back to my suite and rocked my world."

"What can I say? I've always been a sucker for a hot guy."

Damien grinned. "Good, then spread your legs nice and wide for big daddy."

Chapter 10

A mellow, golden light spilled into the master bedroom, but it was the sound of the storm door banging against the frame that woke Niveah up. Trying to remember how she'd ended up in bed, she rolled onto her back and stretched her hands above her head. Damien must have carried her upstairs, because there was no way she had been strong enough to walk on her own.

A few hours ago, Damien had whispered goodbye in her ear. She had a vague recollection of him playing with her hair and kissing her on the lips, but as she thought more about it, she realized how implausible it was. That wasn't Damien. He wasn't the romantic type. Like her, he was looking for a good time and nothing more.

Niveah rolled out of bed. It hurt to move, and every muscle in her body ached. Why had she let Damien convince her to try something new? The next time he suggested they try the Joystick Joyride, she was faking a headache. The position called for extreme flexibility, and she'd had to call on everything she'd learned in gymnastics to keep from crashing to the floor.

The scent of passion fruit was heavy in the air, causing her to wonder if Damien had showered before he left. As she hobbled down the stairs, she glanced out the window. Free from clouds, the sky was clear and blue. Next door, children splashed in a kiddie pool, playing and laughing gleefully. It was the perfect day to kick back at the beach, but Niveah had no plans to sunbathe. There was work to be done on the S.W.A.G. campaign and no time to waste.

Desperate for a cup of hot coffee, she entered the kitchen and headed straight for the coffeemaker. Niveah's eyes widened and her jaw dropped. Positioned on the island next to the fruit bowl was a lavish gift basket. Bubbling with excitement, she ripped open the cellophane and inspected each item. The package of chocolate-covered marshmallows. The sixteen-ounce mug with the words "Boss Lady" splashed across it. The box of edible condoms. Stuffed with an assortment of gourmet foods and a dozen brands of imported coffee, the gift basket looked expensive and smelled divine. How had Damien pulled this off?

Niveah reached for the cordless phone. There was only one way to find out. While she waited for the call to connect, she ripped open the bag of macadamia nuts and tossed some into her mouth. "Hello? Damien?"

"I'm sorry, but he's not available right now."

Niveah tensed at the sound of the woman's voice. Was she his lover? A live-in girlfriend? Last night, Damien told her he was single, but now some chick was answering his cell phone. Add to that, she sounded like a teenager. What was with all these men chasing after young girls? First her ex and now Damien. Realizing she was jumping to conclusions, she shelved the thought. "Okay, thanks. I'll try him again later—"

Silence followed, then she heard a loud rustling sound. "Hello, Niveah?"

"Oh, hey, Damien. Am I catching you at a bad time?"

"No, not at all. What's up?"

Niveah thought of asking Damien who had answered his phone, but decided against it. "I'm just calling to thank you for the gift basket."

"You're welcome. Did you enjoy your breakfast?"

"I haven't made anything to eat yet. I saw the basket and called you right away."

"Check inside the microwave."

"Why?" she asked, glancing at it. "I don't understand."

"Woman, just do what you're told. I'll wait."

When Niveah opened the microwave door, the scent of Italian sausages hit her nostrils. Licking her lips, she lifted the plate and set it down on the counter. The food was arranged in a smiley face, and made her laugh. "I can't believe you went to all this trouble for me."

"I hope the sausages weren't too crispy. I like mine burnt, but I didn't think you would."

"I didn't even know you could cook. I thought you lived on takeout."

"Most of the time I do!"

Niveah tasted the waffles. "Ummm... Damien, this is *really* good. I can't wait to see what you whip up next."

"This is a one-time treat," he announced, turning serious. "The truth is, I rarely step into the kitchen. I think it's something in my genes, because there's a whole line of Hunter men who can't boil water!"

They laughed.

"So you've never made breakfast for a woman before?"

"Nope, you're the first."

It took a moment for her to realize the magnitude of his confession. Did that mean that she was special? That he cared about her in some little way? Niveah refused to entertain the thought. Damien was a player, a skirt chaser, a man who loved sex but didn't do relationships, and that was never going to change. "I don't know what to say."

"Say you'll go with me to the For Lovers Only party at Mystic tonight. It's been sold out for months, but I have a friend who owes me a favor, and he promised me two tickets."

The thought of going dancing with him excited her, but Niveah knew it was a bad idea. Located on a street packed with high-end bars, Mystic was arguably the most exclusive nightclub in town and popular among her staff. What if someone spotted them together and word got back to her boss? Niveah shuddered. Attending the party with Damien was out of the question. If she wanted to become vice president, she had to keep her eyes on the prize.

"I wish I could go, but I still haven't finalized the online ads and internet spots for S.W.A.G.," she explained, cutting up her blueberry waffle. "The photo shoot is next week and I'll have to brief Kenyon Blake on what the visual theme is for the line."

"You're not going to make me go alone, are you? That's just cruel."

A picture of Damien sprang into her mind. She could see him now: furrowed eyebrows, bottom lip poking out, sad, woeful eyes. And just when Niveah thought he couldn't sound any unhappier, his voice sunk another miserable notch.

"I'll be the only one without a date, and everyone will be staring at me. Do you want that on your conscience?"

Niveah tried not to laugh, but she did. When it came to Damien, she had absolutely no willpower. Since meeting him, she'd developed a bad habit of caving in to his every request. It was pathetic, really. And if she didn't nip it in the bud now, she'd be kicking herself later. "I can't, Damien. I need to get these ads done today, and I'm already behind as it is."

"I'm going out of town for a few days, and I really want see you before I leave. Honor a traveling man's final request."

"And they say women are dramatic."

"I'm not being dramatic. It's the truth. We need to hook up."

It was hard, but Niveah held her ground. "I have to pull the rest of the ad campaign together, but we'll hang out when you come back. I promise."

"Or I can give you a hand on the ads this afternoon, and we can party tonight."

"But you hate going to the office on weekends."

"Who said anything about going downtown? We'll work at your house."

Glancing into the living room brought memories of last night. They'd made love twice, three times if you counted the orgasm she'd had when Damien buried his face between her legs. For the second time in weeks, he had exceeded her expectations in the foreplay department, and just thinking about the way he'd pleased her made Niveah's legs tingle. The chances of them getting work done at her house was as likely as a plus-size woman being featured on the cover of *Vogue* magazine, but she found herself slowly warming to the idea. "I don't know about this. I do my best work at the office."

"Eat your breakfast, because you're going to need your strength," he told her, his tone thick with sexual innuendo. "I plan to work you like you've never been worked before."

"Do you always have sex on the brain?"

"Only when it comes to you."

Charged up by their racy conversation, she swiped a glass from the dish rack, filled it with cold water, and gulped some down. Working on the ad campaign with Damien was becoming stressful, but she refused to bow to the pressure. After all, she was a professional. A highly talented creative director who never missed a deadline or disappointed her clients. She was going to get the internet ads done today, come hell or high water.

"You worry too much. We'll get it done."

He spoke with assurance, confidence—an optimism that Niveah didn't feel.

"Let me think about it," she said, hoping to buy herself some time. "I'll call you back in twenty minutes. Are you still staying at the hotel?"

"No, I just bought a place in the Beach Park Isles area. But don't bother calling me back."

"Why not?"

"Because I'm making an executive decision. I'll see you in an hour!"

Long after their conversation ended, Niveah was still thinking about Damien. Seated on the couch, eating the breakfast he'd prepared for her, she found herself wondering who the woman was who answered his phone. They'd had sex twice, but that didn't give her the license to question him. What he did in his free time was none of her business, right?

Niveah wondered what her friends would say when she told them what happened last night with Damien. They'd probably break out in cheers. All Roxi talked about these days was finding her soul mate, and just yesterday she'd announced, "If I don't find Mr. Right this year, I'm moving to Texas. They have tons of eligible bachelors, and I hear they're ripe for the picking!"

Instead of joining the discussion, she'd advised Roxi to concentrate less on finding a man and more on advancing her career. That had been Niveah's goal since the day she left Chickasaw, and each promotion only fueled her desire to succeed. Adamant about gaining her independence, she'd bought a one-way ticket to Tampa when she turned eighteen. There were many challenges during her first year away from home, but she'd refused to give up. Enrolling in college had changed her life for the better, and two years after graduating with an associate's degree in finance, she was hired at Access

Media and Entertainment. Once on staff, there'd been no stopping her. If she could make something out of her life, anyone could. That's the message she shared with the girls she mentored, and she hoped they took her words to heart.

Still thinking about her conversation yesterday with Roxi, she forked some breakfast potatoes into her mouth. It amazed her that so many intelligent, college-educated women were holding out for Prince Charming. There was no such thing. Hadn't Hollywood proven that, time and time again? She wasn't buying into the whole everyone-has-a-soul-mate belief, either. Niveah didn't need a man to validate her, and she felt pity for those who did. She had it going on, and if the opposite sex didn't realize it, it was their loss. That's why she refused to lament her breakup with Stewart. He was a louse, a liar, a cheater of the worse kind. Instead of talking to her about their problems, he'd found solace in the arms of a chesty bimbo. Returning his engagement ring had been a no-brainer, and after Niveah donated everything he'd left at her house to Goodwill, she'd felt a hundred times better.

Niveah gulped down the rest of her coffee, stood and put her dishes in the sink. She had a date—correction—a business meeting to get ready for, and no time to waste. Deciding what to wear wasn't going to be easy, and as she climbed the staircase, she wondered what Damien would do if she answered the door in her silk teddy. A giggle bubbled up in her throat. What had gotten into her? First she'd agreed to work with Damien at home, knowing full well nothing would get done, and now she was fantasizing about seducing him.

And then there was their date tonight. Deep down she wanted to attend the For Lovers Only party with him. What better way to spend Valentine's Day than in the arms of a tall, gorgeous man? Falling for Damien wasn't an option, but as Niveah stepped into the shower and turned the water on full blast, she feared she'd bitten off more than she could chew.

Chapter 11

At three o'clock on Friday afternoon, Damien strode into the downtown studio where the S.W.A.G. photo shoot was taking place. He'd come straight from the airport, and although he wasn't required to be there, he felt it was important he show his face.

Seeing Niveah has nothing to do with it, he told himself. After all, they weren't a couple. They were just kicking it. That's why it didn't bother him that Niveah hadn't returned any of his calls while he was away. His trip back east had been a bust, but he'd find a way to fix the problems in his family even if it killed him.

Inside the brick building, the production staff was scurrying around moving props. He was poised, relaxed, in total command of himself and his emotions. Without slowing, he greeted everyone he passed with a nod and a smile. Where was Niveah? Surely she was around here somewhere. They hadn't talked all week, and Damien was more than a little anxious to see her. As he searched the room for the bombshell businesswoman with the enticing shape, he grooved to the R & B song playing on the radio.

Damien stopped at the refreshment table. Trays filled with sandwiches, vegetables and fruit caught his eye, The scent of fresh cantaloupe reminded him of the last time he'd seen Niveah. A grin overwhelmed his mouth. They never did make it to the For Lovers Only concert. Damien didn't know if it was because she smelled good or because of how sexy she looked in her blue jeans, but he couldn't stop himself from touching her.

Convinced he heard her voice, he turned around. Stunned by what he saw, he stopped abruptly in the middle of the lounge. Damien couldn't believe his eyes. Niveah was wearing a dress. A sexy, sleeveless number that showed off her trim, chocolate-brown legs. And that wasn't all. She was wearing makeup and accessories, and her hair was styled in an ultrastraight bob that grazed her shoulders.

Damien felt an erection tent in his pants. Wondering if there were any offices in the back where they could sneak off for a quickie, he tried to catch Niveah's attention. His temperature rose, and a searing heat rushed to his groin. Perspiring like a sheik in the Arabian desert, Damien greedily gulped in air. He had to have her. Here. Now. Before he exploded in his dress pants.

Taking a deep breath didn't help him regain control. Damien wondered if they made a patch for what he had. This wasn't him, but since meeting Niveah he'd been doing things he wouldn't normally do. Like right now. He was standing in the middle of the room wondering what kind of panties she was wearing under her dress. And once he got her away from that pretty-boy photographer she was talking to, he was going to find out.

Damien scowled when he saw Niveah place a hand on Kenyon Blake's forearm. The lump in his throat threatened to choke him, and loosening his tie didn't alleviate the pressure.

Badly in need of a drink, he swiped a soda off the refreshment table, pulled back the tab, and gulped it down. Damien was glad he wasn't the jealous type. If he was, he would have stormed over to the pair and pulled Niveah away.

Is this why Niveah hadn't returned any of my calls? Because she was too busy hanging out with the celebrity photographer? Damien had never met Kenyon Blake, but he instantly disliked him. *This has gone on long enough,* he decided, draining his can. More nervous than a groom on his wedding day, he cleaned the sweat from his hands and squared his shoulders. *Enough standing around, it's time to break this up.*

"How long have you been sweet on Niveah?"

Damien hung his head. He didn't have to look over his shoulder to know that Terrence Franklin and Rashawn "The Glove" Bishop were standing on either side of him. "It's good to see you guys," he lied, producing a smile.

"It looks like we showed up right in the nick of time." Terrence shoved another soda into his hand. "Chill, D. They're just discussing the photo shoot."

"What are you talking about, man? I'm not interested in her romantically. It's just sex. Great sex mind you, but nothing more."

Rashawn slanted his eyebrows. "Right, and I love long walks and heartfelt talks!"

Damien chuckled. "Is your wife still forcing you to attend those couple-retreats in the mountains? You said you were going to put your foot down. What happened?"

"Actually, Yasmin's pregnant with our second child, so she's slowed down some."

"My wife's in her last trimester, and she's on strict bed rest. Needless to say, things have been crazy around our house."

Damien clapped a hand on his friend's back. "Damn, Terrence, every time I see you you're expecting. How many kids do you have now? Seven? Eight?"

The footballer chuckled. "Only two. A girl and a boy."

"Only two?" Rashawn whistled. "You're not planning on having your own little league football team, are you, man?"

The men laughed heartedly.

"I want to thank you guys again for doing this ad campaign," Damien said. "When you return to town for the big S.W.A.G. launch in June I'll treat you and your wives to dinner."

"Will you be bringing Niveah along?"

"You know I'm not the type to be tied to one woman."

"I'm worried about you, man. You have this wild, murderous look on your face, and the veins in your neck are throbbing like crazy," Terrence pointed out. "You're jealous that Niveah's talking to Kenyon Blake, aren't you?"

Damien ignored the question. "If you guys are done shooting your spot, we can bounce. It's been a while since we hung out. Let's catch up over a game of pool and some beer."

"If you're payin', I'm playin'."

"Just give me a minute to check in with my wife," Rashawn said, opening his cell phone.

"Check in?" Damien laughed hard. "I never thought I'd see the day where you'd be answering to a woman."

"If Yasmin's happy, then I'm happy. She's my world, and I'm not going to do anything to jeopardize the good thing we've got going."

Terrence agreed. "Go ahead and school the young pup. I've got your back."

"I was like you once, a long, *long* time ago. I thought love was for suckers, thought giving my heart to someone would make me soft, make me less of a man." Rashawn sounded somber. "But then I met Yasmin and my opinion changed. It's like I was living in the dark and she came along to show me the light."

"Man, you sound like one of those weepy dudes in those corny greeting card commercials."

"Well, that makes two of us, because reuniting with my

college sweetheart was the best thing that ever happened to me," Terrence admitted. "It's the greatest feeling in the world to know you have a woman in your life who's a hundred percent behind you. Kyra's made me a better man, and I don't know what I'd do without her."

Damien's gaze drifted back across the room to where Niveah was standing. She was still chatting it up with the photographer. They were standing so close he'd need the Jaws of Life to separate them. Damien told himself he didn't care, told himself he had better things to do with his time than hang around the photo studio. Besides, catching feelings for Niveah would only complicate matters. He liked their arrangement just the way it was. No emotions, no heartache. Love was for the birds, and as long as he remembered that he'd be fine. "I plan to be a lifelong bachelor, and there's nothing either of you can say to change my mind. It's like my boy Eric Benet said, 'Love just don't love me'."

His friends scoffed.

"If I had a dollar for every time I heard one of my boys say that—"

"I could afford to buy the Starbucks franchise!" Rashawn gave Terrence a pound. "You haven't met the right woman yet, but when you do nothing else will matter."

"Thanks for the talk, Dr. Phil, but I've been burned enough to know that I'm better off alone." Damien laughed, but even as the words left his mouth, he knew they weren't true.

It's official, Niveah thought, closing her eyes and massaging her temples with her fingertips. *My career just crashed and burned.* How could so many things go wrong in one day? The morning had started off with an irate phone call from her boss, and had gotten progressively worse as the photo shoot dragged on. The only bright spot of the day had been meeting Kenyon Blake.

"Are we ready to roll?"

Niveah turned around and smiled apologetically at the world-renowned photographer with the smoldering eyes. "Mr. Blake, I am so sorry about all of the unnecessary delays. Things usually run a lot smoother than this on my projects."

"Don't sweat it, and please call me Kenyon."

"I don't know what I'm going to do if the last model doesn't show," she said, glancing at the door. "I've called the Euphoria agency a half dozen times, but no one's picking up."

"Try not to worry." Kenyon slid a hand into the pocket of his jeans. "And if you're worried about running over budget, I can waive the afternoon's fees."

"I couldn't let you do that. We have a contract, and I'm going to honor it."

"As far as I'm concerned, meeting my favorite running back is payment enough. Terrence Franklin was cool enough to sign my T-shirt, and asked for my number so I could take photos of his new baby next month."

Niveah glanced over at the refreshment table. The former NFL superstar was surrounded by an awestruck group of admirers, and cracking jokes with Tampa's golden boy, Rashawn "The Glove" Bishop. The boxer had caused quite a stir when he arrived at the studio an hour ago. And despite the fact that he was wearing a platinum wedding band, women knocked each other over trying to reach him. "I'm worried that we're not going to finish on time."

"Don't be. We're almost done."

"I know, but the shoot was only supposed to take a couple hours, not six."

"Normally, I wouldn't mind staying an extra day or two, but I'm flying out tonight. My wife's on assignment in Prague and she's expecting me there in the morning."

"Is she a model?"

"She could be." A proud smile sat on his lips. "Makayla's a teacher, but she decided to take a break to pursue her dream of being a travel writer. Reading her articles are the highlight of my week, and I couldn't be more proud of her."

Listening to Kenyon Blake made Niveah reflect on past relationships. None of her ex-boyfriends had ever gushed about her. Not a single one. Would she ever meet a man who adored her? And love her the way her dad did her mom? "I look forward to meeting your wife at the launch party, Kenyon. I know you're incredibly busy, but I'm expecting you both to be there."

Niveah's breath caught when Damien crossed her line of vision. Her gaze trailed him around the room. He looked calm, relaxed, as if he'd spent the last ten days at a luxury spa. Or in the hands of a very flexible geisha. She watched him, spellbound by how effortlessly he connected with the people around him. Even though Damien drove her crazy at work, it was good to have him back. His absence had been felt by everyone, and just that morning she'd heard staff members discussing his return. The creative team was eagerly awaiting his arrival, and for good reason. Damien filled the group with enthusiasm, gave everyone the freedom to be themselves and was always quick to laugh. And it didn't hurt that he was hot, too.

Niveah had to talk to him. He'd know what to do about the absentee model. *Hell, he should just take the guy's place,* she thought, admiring how drop-dead gorgeous he looked in his casual attire. Damien should be cloned, she decided, licking her lips. He was every woman's dream. Attractive, successful and more charismatic than a politician. With that disarming grin, those dreamy eyes, and the hardware he was packing below the belt, Damien deserved his own feature spread in the S.W.A.G. calendar.

While Kenyon talked about the various lighting adjustments that needed to be made before the next shoot, Niveah snuck covert glances at Damien. He was talking to his celebrity friends, but when the group separated minutes later, she made her move. "Kenyon, I'll be right back. The other creative director is here, and I want to pick his brain about the photo shoot."

"No problem, I'll be waiting on the set if you need me."

Moving as fast as her high heels could take her, she hustled across the room, reaching Damien in five seconds flat. "I know you're on your way out," she said, tapping him on the shoulder. "But can I talk to you for a moment?"

Damien turned around and blessed her with his sweet-as-sugar smile. "I'm surprised you even noticed I was here."

His eyes bore down on her, making it impossible for Niveah speak. Seeing him again excited her. All week she'd been desperate to hear his voice, but she had been too proud to call. Doing so would suggest that she missed him, and since they weren't exclusive she had no business blowing up his phone.

"Guys, give me a few minutes," he said, glancing over his shoulder at his friends. After promising to meet them outside, Damien took Niveah by the arm and led her to a quiet corner, away from the crowd. "How have you been?"

"Insanely busy. I've been helping the teenagers I mentor prep for their final exams, and I've been at the office until midnight practically every day this week."

"I didn't ask you about work. I asked how *you* were doing."

"Damien, when it comes to my life, they're one and the same."

"No they're not, but don't worry I'm here to show you the difference." The tone of his voice was light, but his gaze was intense. "You look great. You're wearing the hell out of that dress, and I love what you've done to your hair."

"It's amazing, you always know just what to say," she said, poking him in the shoulder. "When you're tired of the advertising business, you should consider a career in politics."

"I will if you promise to be my first lady."

Niveah concealed a smile. She'd love to spend the rest of the afternoon flirting with Damien, but she had more problems than an award-winning rapper charged with drug possession, and she needed to focus on saving the photo shoot. "Damien, I'm in trouble and I really need your help."

He moved closer. "It sounds serious. What's going on?"

"One of the models is a no-show."

"Have you tried calling his agency?"

Niveah nodded. "Only a dozen times. No one's answering the phone."

"I can drive over there if you think that will help."

"There's no time. Kenyon's only here until five."

"Kenyon, huh?" Furrowing his eyebrows, he rubbed a hand slowly over his goatee. On the face of it, Niveah seemed genuinely excited to see him, but he couldn't help wondering if it was all an act. After all, he hadn't heard from her in days. "What's going on with you two?" he asked, trying to sound casual. "Have you guys been kicking it while I was away?"

"Kenyon's happily married."

"He's married?" Damien chuckled. "Well, that's the best news I've heard all day!"

Unsure of what to make of his comment, she steered the conversation back to the troubled photo shoot. "I need a huge favor."

"What is it? You know I'll do anything to help out."

"Fill in for the missing model, so we can wrap up this photo shoot today."

The carefree expression on his face dissolved.

"I've called every modeling agency I've ever heard of, but no one's available until tomorrow, and we need to get this shoot in the bag today." Another thought came to mind, one that made her jealous, but was sure to persuade him to do the ad. "Think of all the attention you'll be bringing to the agency when the calendar is released this fall. Women will be chasing you down the street to get your autograph."

The lines around Damien's mouth hardened. He didn't know why, but her comment annoyed him. The truth was, chasing skirts wasn't as fun as it used to be. Seducing attractive women used to be his favorite pastime, but lately he'd lost interest in the whole cat-and-mouse game. Damien didn't know if he felt like torching his black book because he'd met Niveah or because… A frown gripped his lips. Why couldn't he think of another reason? Something other than him being smitten with his gorgeous colleague?

"You've got the right look, Damien. You're tall, perfectly groomed, and you'll photograph well," she said, her voice earnest and sincere. "And we have wardrobe in your size. All you have to do is go into the dressing room, run past makeup and…"

"Niveah, I can't." Casting his eyes around the room, he shuffled his feet as if he was doing the Texas two-step. "I'm more of a behind-the-scenes type of guy. I want to help out, but—"

"I never pegged you as the shy type."

Damien scratched his neck. "I'm not, I just…getting in front of the camera is not me."

"What if I made a thousand-dollar donation to your favorite charity? It's Huntington's Disease of America, right?" Sensing that he was on the verge of conceding, Niveah linked arms with him. "Please, Damien? You'd be saving my butt *and* the S.W.A.G. ad campaign."

The protective armor around his heart melted to a pool at his feet. Niveah's beautiful, brown eyes were filled with hope and he didn't want to disappoint her. "Okay, okay, I'll do it."

Niveah threw her arms around his neck. "Damien, thank you so much! I don't know how I'm ever going to repay you!"

"I do. We're going out tonight."

"I can't. I'm having drinks with a prospective client."

Realizing he finally had the upper hand made him smile. "Cancel. I want to go to the hockey game, and you're going to be my date."

"We'll go out tomorrow. I promise."

"No," he said, drawing out the word. "We're hanging out tonight. This is my last chance to see the Tampa Bay Lightning play this season, and I'm really looking forward to it."

Clutching his forearm like an Egyptian drowning in the Red Sea, she made a desperate plea for understanding. "Be reasonable, Damien. You don't expect me to blow off my out-of-town clients, do you?"

"You've been running around here like a madwoman all day, and you deserve the night off. Let's go out and have a good time. You've earned it, boss lady."

"What am I supposed to tell Mr. Kumar and his associates?"

Amusement shone in his eyes as he spoke. "Tell them your business hours are from nine and five and you'd be happy to reschedule during work hours."

"I can't do that!"

"My terms are simple. No date, no photo." Damien made a show of staring at his gold watch. "But if we're going to do this it's got to be now, because time is running out."

"Are you blackmailing me?"

Behind them, something crashed to the floor, and the room erupted in chaos. To be heard above the clamor, Damien lowered his mouth, brushing it every so lightly against the gentle curve of her ear. "Yes, in fact I am. And you know what, *Ms. Evans?* It feels damn good."

Chapter 12

"I never imagined I'd have this much fun at a hockey game," Niveah confessed, waving her Tampa Bay Lightning towel wildly in the air. The arena was a sea of blue T-shirts, children clutched homemade signs and the overzealous announcer implored the crowd to get "fired up."

"These fans are incredible. They really go all out for the home team."

"This is nothing. You should see what happens during the playoffs!"

For the last forty minutes, they'd cheered on the home team and banged on the Plexiglas like the drunken college students sitting beside them. Niveah was having a great time, but the best part of the night wasn't the action on the ice. It was learning more about Damien. At the office he was the center of attention, but here, alone—just with her—he was easygoing and relaxed. From their conversation, she learned that he had traveled to more than fifty countries, was passionate about giving back to the community and was a sports fanatic. But what surprised Niveah more than anything was how much he loved his parents.

"You didn't finish telling me about your…" Niveah trailed off when the crowd erupted in cheers. The buzzer sounded, signaling the end of the second period. Fans filed out of the arena, and headed toward the concession stands. "Tell me more about your father's NFL career."

Damien leaned back in his seat, a pensive expression on his face. "My dad was one of the fastest big men to ever play the game. His nickname was, 'The Human Wrecking Machine', and the fifteen seasons he played with the New York Giants made him an international superstar. Back in the day we couldn't go anywhere without being mobbed."

"It must have been tough sharing your dad with the world."

"I was too proud of him to notice!" He laughed, but when he spoke again his tone was quiet, muted, as if each word was a struggle. "My dad wasn't around much when I was growing up, but he was a terrific father. It didn't matter what city he was playing in, he always called every night to see how I was doing. When I got into the advertising field, I promised myself I would never to use his celebrity to advance my career, but his positive reputation has definitely helped me along the way. He's an incredible man, everything I ever hope to be."

"I'm sure you've made your father very proud, Damien. You're a great guy, and I'm not just saying that because you bailed me out this afternoon. You…"

Niveah faltered over her words when Damien touched her. His hand, resting casually on her thigh, warmed her from the inside out. Struck by the remarkable depths of his eyes, she openly admired his thick eyebrows and dimpled chin.

To regain focus, she cleared all thoughts of kissing him out of her mind. "After all those years of getting banged up on the football field, your dad must really be enjoying his retirement."

Sadness flashed across his face. "It's been different that's for sure. Speaking of parents, when are Ma and Pa Evans coming to town?"

"Quit calling them that," she ordered, trying not to laugh. "They'll be here in two weeks."

"Are you excited?"

Scared Damien would detect that she was lying, she nodded and stared out onto the rink. In light of what he'd just told her about his family, she knew he wouldn't understand her love-hate relationship with her parents. Niveah adored her mom and dad, but she could only handle them in small doses. Christmas. Easter. Fourth of July. Spending ten days with her mom was going to drive her to the brink—of alcohol or depression, she didn't know. Her parents had a knack for embarrassing her, for drawing huge laughs from strangers in public; but this time Niveah wasn't having it. The second her parents acted country she was pulling the plug on the whole trip.

"They've never been to Tampa, so it should be fun. I have a long list of places I want to take them, but with everything I have going on at the office, it's going to be hard to leave early."

"I can hardly wait to meet them."

Niveah cranked her head in his direction. "Well, *that's* not going to happen."

"Man, you're cold." Placing a hand on his chest, he groaned as if he'd been struck by a bullet. "I know why you don't want me to meet your parents. You're scared they'll fall in love with me and no man will ever be able to measure up to me in the future, right?"

"Yeah, that's it, Damien. You figured it out."

Chuckling, he flagged down a vendor with eighties-style hair. "Over here, man."

A minute later, Niveah bit into the thickest, juiciest hotdog she'd ever seen. "This is *so* good." A sigh of utter delight fell from her lips. "I've put on five pounds since we started dating, and if you keep feeding me like this, I'll have to buy a new wardrobe!"

"Is this what we're doing? Dating?"

Niveah's cheeks burned. It was a foot-in-the mouth moment, one she'd do anything to undo. "That came out wrong. What I meant was—"

"No, it's cool, if that's what you want. Is it?"

"I don't know."

"You don't know? Funny, I never pegged you as the shy type."

A scowl clung to Niveah's lips. "God, I hate when you do that."

"Do what? Quote you?"

"Yeah. It's annoying."

"Quit playing," he teased, grinning. "You know you love it."

You're right. I do. Niveah had gather her wits, had to stop flirting with him. They were wrong for each other. All wrong. And indulging in a sleazy office affair would not only ruin her chances of landing the VP position, it would lead to heartbreak. Although she'd been the one to proposition him on New Year's Eve, she wasn't cut out for casual hookups, and Damien had made it clear he wasn't interested in a serious commitment. "I like hanging out with you, Damien. You're outgoing and funny and—"

"Don't forget sexy," he added, in a mock serious tone. "You probably don't know this, but the women at the office call me the black McDreamy."

Niveah laughed so hard tears trickled down her cheeks. "You're too much."

"I know. It's a good thing I finally found a sister strong enough to keep me in line, huh?"

Then, he leaned over, and kissed her so passionately she moaned.

Damien's red car was the only one in the arena parking lot, but when they exited the stairwell, he took Niveah's hand and drew her close. It was a sweet, romantic gesture, one that made her feel safe.

"I can't believe it's almost midnight," Niveah said, zipping up her jacket.

After the game, Damien had insisted on taking her to the chic restaurant lounge on the upper deck, and they'd sat in a cozy booth talking until closing time. "I should have been in bed hours ago. I have a six a.m. conference call with Mrs. Garrett-Reed in the morning."

"We should play hooky from work tomorrow."

"Don't you think it'll raise suspicions if we both call in sick?"

"I doubt it, but even if it does, who cares? Life's about living in the moment, Niveah, not following rules." Damien wore a wry expression. "Did you have fun at the game?"

"I sure did. Thanks to you, I was able to enjoy myself instead of fretting about all the work left to do on the S.W.A.G. ad campaign."

"I'm a pretty decent guy, huh?"

"The best. And you were incredible on the set this afternoon." Images of Damien's sexy photo shoot came to mind. Standing in the shadows, watching him pose for the cameras in nothing but black pajama bottoms had given her heart palpitations. And when Niveah glanced around the studio she noticed that she wasn't the only woman battling a serious case of lust. "You should have seen the looks on the faces of the female staff when you stepped out of your dressing room. They were drooling all over their J. Crew twin sets!"

"And they say men are dogs."

"Most of them are." She hastened to add, "Present company excluded of course."

Damien stopped walking. He stood in the middle of the parking garage just staring at her. Niveah was too uptight about work and strived for perfection in every aspect of her life, but she was the most authentic woman he had ever met. And he loved how she kept him in check. She wasn't afraid to disagree with him, or put him in his place and that was damn hot. "Tell me again how much you missed me."

"It wasn't the same around the office without you."

His eyes settled on her lips. "What exactly did you miss?"

"Everything. Talking to you, laughing with you, arguing."

"Is that all?"

"No, there were a few other things," she said, her tone sultry.

"Show me."

Nothing excited Niveah more than a challenge. Proving that she could be every bit as bold as he was, she kissed him hard on the lips. She savored his scent, the taste of his lips, and the feel of his tongue inside her mouth. The parking garage was deathly quiet, but soon their frantic moans and heavy breathing filled the air.

"Let's go back to your crib." Damien pointed his key at the car and the doors unlocked.

"But your place is closer."

"I'm still moving in. The house is a mess."

"I don't care."

"It wouldn't be safe. I'm having work done in the kitchen

and there are tools and machines everywhere." He slid his hand down her back and grabbed her butt with both hands. "Now get your pretty little ass in the car before I do you right here."

"Promise?" Niveah squeezed his biceps. Desperate for him, she nipped and sucked and teased his tongue into her mouth. Pressed flat against his chest, she ran her hands down his hard, muscular shoulders. Damien backed her up against the car, a hungry, desperate look in his eyes. He was a live grenade. Up for anything, always willing, impulsive and wild. Why not show him that she could be spontaneous, too?

Using her nipples to caress his chest brought out the beast in him. He growled savagely in her ear, cursed and grunted. It was time to move in for the kill. Forsaking everything she'd ever learned in church about modesty and decorum, she hiked her leg around his waist and rocked her hips to the erotic rap beat playing in her mind.

Damien plunged a hand inside her top, and when a breast popped out of her bra, he eagerly sucked it into his mouth. Waves of pleasure overtook her, making her feel lightheaded and dizzy. Niveah closed her eyes until the moment passed. Things had quickly gone from PG to X-rated, but the prospect of having sex in public excited her. Tonight, she wasn't the uptight creative director people disliked, she was an erotic, sensuous woman who Damien desired.

Grinning as if she had a secret that she was unwilling to share, Niveah reached between his legs and seized his erection. The look of surprise on his face was a turn-on, more arousing than the fiery French kisses they'd shared moments earlier.

As if seated on a stool, she squatted, unzipped his pants, and yanked down his boxer briefs. Niveah held his shaft in one hand, and massaged the tip with the other. The first flick of her tongue made him groan. The second caused his eyes to roll in the back of his head. And by the time she sucked him into her mouth he was chanting her name.

Niveah slowed down her pace. Damien was breathing hard, deeply, through his nose, as if he was on the verge of passing out. But then he was groaning, grunting, thrusting himself deeper inside her mouth. She saw the fire in his eyes, and felt prouder than a gold medalist standing on the Olympic podium.

To delay his orgasm, he pulled his erection out of her mouth, leaving just the tip for her to suck on. He ran his hands through her hair and watched as the long, silky strands fell through his fingers. The way Niveah moved her hands and mouth was truly a sight to behold. The sister had a cornucopia of sexual moves, techniques that left him gasping for each breath. And when she licked from his erection to his navel and back again, a shudder racked his body. Then, as if that wasn't enough, she drew her teeth down the length of his shaft. There was no denying it, no play acting, no frontin' any more. Niveah was his weakness, his kryptonite, the only woman he couldn't resist. He felt weak but oddly exhilarated.

Cupping her head, he bent down and kissed her deeply on the lips. Enough was enough. It was time to show this woman what he was all about. Niveah spread her hands on the hood of his car and batted her eyelashes at him. In a throaty whisper she said, "I hope you're not going to frisk me, Officer."

Damien cracked a sly smile. He wished he had a video camera, wished he could capture this moment, because seeing Niveah bent over the hood of his car was something he'd love to see on his sixty-inch screen TV. It was hard to believe that this was the same woman his colleagues called the "Heart of Darkness." *If these walls could only talk.*

Niveah poked her bottom in the air, as if issuing another challenge. He needed a minute to catch his breath, didn't she? *A Red Bull would come in handy right now,* he thought, massaging her big, juicy butt.

"I-I-I can't take it anymore. I feel like I'm going to burst," she panted, throwing her head back against his chest. "Do me now, baby. *Right now.*"

Desire ruled him like a slave to its master. In one swift motion, he pulled down her panties and plunged into her. He felt her tightness all around him. Fast and furious he moved inside her. She bucked against him, imploring him to make deeper, longer strokes. Gripping her hips, he spread his legs wide and thrust to the beat of her groans. An intense pressure settled in his groin. The sensation was so powerful, so devastating he thought his heart would quit.

When the distant sound of footsteps reached Damien's ears, he stopped moving. Narrowing his eyes, he slowly glanced around the deserted garage. Nothing. Was his mind playing tricks on him or was some pervert watching them from behind one of the pillars?

"Did you hear that?" Niveah's head whipped up. Staring at him over her shoulder, strands of hair clinging to her face, she looked incredibly sexy. "Someone's coming."

"So am I." One final thrust and he collapsed beside her on the hood of his car. The orgasm knocked him over, battered him like a debilitated ship in the eye of a storm. Niveah's light touch to the side of his face calmed him, allowed his mind to clear.

Lifting his head, he stroked her hair as if it was the finest silk. Damien told himself that this was just sex, that his feelings for Niveah were clouded by the monstrous orgasm he'd just had, but when she kissed him his heart softened like whipped butter.

Smiling, his chest puffed up with pride, he closed his arms around her. He'd lusted after this woman for weeks, and now that they were finally exclusive, he didn't ever want to let her go. She'd touched his life in a very real way, made him a happier, more fulfilled man, and he was grateful to have found her. Damien hung his head. Damn, now *he* sounded like one of those corny dudes in a card commercial.

"I could stay here with you like this forever."

Damien chuckled. "Really? In the arena parking lot?"

"You know what I mean."

He paused, and gave some thought to what she said. Damien parted his lips, but couldn't make his mouth form the words that his heart wanted to say. "I'd better take you home. You have a long day ahead of you tomorrow."

"Why don't you sleep at my place? That way you wouldn't have to drive back across town."

"Thanks, but I can't. I have an early morning meeting, too."

"I understand." She didn't, but she decided not to argue. Niveah didn't know why, but it bothered her that he never spent the night at her house. Within an hour of making love, he was showered, dressed and back out the door. "Damien, is there someone else?"

Holding her gaze, he spoke in a quiet whisper, as if they were surrounded by a roomful of people who might overhear. "I come across strong sometimes, especially because I'm really feeling you, but I'm not a player. I don't lie, I don't cheat and I don't dog sisters out. I've been upfront with you from the beginning, and that's not going to change."

"You're always in a rush to leave my place after we make love, and I thought maybe it was because you had another woman in your life."

"Where is this coming from? I thought we were having a good time. You know? Keeping things casual, not stressing each other out, not making this more than what it is?"

Niveah started to speak, then stopped. No sense making

herself look stupid by asking a question she already knew the answer to. "We are. I was just…wondering."

"You're the only woman I want," he said, nibbling on her neck, "and I don't see that changing for a very long time."

Niveah giggled. "Cut it out, Damien. You know that turns me on."

A door slammed behind them.

"Uh-oh, time to bounce!" Scared that arena security was closing in on them, Damien hurried Niveah inside the car and sped off into the night. His plan was to drop her off and head straight home, but when they arrived at her house thirty-five minutes later, he had a change of heart. Instead of kissing Niveah goodnight, he carried her inside the house, locked the door and finished what they'd started in the arena parking lot.

Chapter 13

Every morning at seven a.m. Niveah drank a cup of strong, black coffee while she reviewed the day's agenda. In all the years she'd been working at Access Media and Entertainment, Niveah had never deviated from her routine, but ever since she started dating Damien she'd been spending less time at the office and more time with him.

The month had been a blur of business meetings and long sweaty nights making love to Damien, and as Niveah joined her team one morning for breakfast, she couldn't help reflecting on how her life had changed for the better.

"That sounds like fun," Niveah told the female copywriter who'd just invited her to the fondue party she was hosting next week. "Count me in. I *love* chocolate!"

"Excellent. I have to run, but we'll talk more later." The brunette waved and rushed off.

"Hey, girl, I didn't expect to see you in here."

Niveah glanced up from her plate. "Why not, Jeanette? Creative directors have to eat, too."

"I know, but *you* never come into the staff room to socialize."

"So I've turned over a new leaf. Sue me."

Silence fell between them and lasted for several long, tense seconds.

"Are your parents arriving tonight?"

"Yeah, they should be here by nine thirty," Niveah said, smothering a yawn with her hands.

"Another late night with you know who?"

Niveah smiled sheepishly. Last night, when Damien had slipped a hand around her waist and ushered her through the sliding glass doors of Fahrenheit 220, Niveah felt as if she'd died and gone to celebrity heaven. But it was meeting Ne-Yo that had been the highlight of the evening. And when the R & B crooner took the stage the crowd went wild. There was more silicone in the club than at a plastic surgery clinic, but Damien had kept his eyes only on her. Ignoring everyone around them, he'd taken her in his arms and held her close as they slow-danced to her favorite song. "We went dancing, and didn't get back to my place until—" Niveah peered her watch "—five hours ago."

"I haven't seen you this happy since…well, never."

"With friends like you, who needs enemies?"

"Don't get all prissy," Jeanette told her. "You know what I mean. Dating Damien's been good for you. You're not stressed out anymore, and you're treating your employees better, too."

Niveah chugged a mouthful of coffee. "And how would you know, Jeanette? It's not like we work in the same department or anything."

"People talk, and the word on the street is that Damien's skills in the bedroom have made you one *very* happy woman. I can't help but agree."

The mug fell from Niveah's hands. She seized Jeanette's

forearm, and dragged her out of the staff room and down the hall. "You have such a big mouth! I knew I shouldn't have confided in you!" she yelled, slamming her office door. "Who did you tell that Damien and I are lovers?"

"No one. People aren't stupid, Niveah. The chemistry between you guys is insane. Hell, a blind man in a coma could see it!" Laughing at her own joke, she hopped onto the desk and fished out some jelly beans from the glass candy dish. "You've done a complete one-eighty since Damien arrived, and it's easy to see why. You're hot for him, and the whole office knows it."

"But we've been very discreet."

"Obviously not discreet enough, because I heard word got to Mr. Russo, too."

Niveah's knees buckled but she didn't fall. "Mr. Russo knows that Damien and I are…lovers?" The room spun faster than an amusement park ride, and Niveah feared she wouldn't be able to keep her breakfast down. "Who told him?"

"Who cares? In the big scheme of things it doesn't really matter, does it?"

"Maybe not to you!" she raged through clenched teeth. "It's not *your* career on the line, it's *mine!* God, I can't believe I was stupid enough to think that no one would find out."

"Well, it probably wasn't a good idea to have sex in his office."

"What did you just say?"

Jeanette tossed a red jelly bean into her mouth. "Apparently, while you and Damien were getting down and dirty in his office, the cleaning crew was outside the door listening."

Niveah groaned. Things couldn't get any worse. A prisoner to her thoughts, she recounted every detail of that infamous Sunday afternoon. Damien had met her at six, and on the way out of the building he asked if they could stop by his office to pick up a file. But once inside, he'd locked the door and started kissing her all over.

"I can't believe someone heard us."

"One of the cleaning ladies told a guy in the mailroom and he passed the story on to a buddy in the design department. Nothing spreads faster than a slice of hot, juicy gossip and by the end of Monday everyone knew." Jeanette shrugged, as if bored with the topic. "I don't understand why you're getting so bent out of shape. Since everyone knows that you and Damien are lovers, you can finally come out of the closet. So to speak."

"We can't do that!" Angry that her friend couldn't see the big picture, Niveah strode over to window, hoping the view of the Tampa skyline would help to calm her. "Jeanette, this isn't a good thing. Now my chances of being promoted are next to nil because my reputation's toast."

"That's bull. You're the best damn creative director this company has ever had, and the higher-ups aren't going to give the VP position to someone else just because they found out you're getting your freak on after hours."

Niveah winced as if she'd stubbed her toe on the side of the desk. Why did Jeanette make her relationship with Damien sound so cheap? So degrading? It was true, they had world-class sex, but that's not the only reason why they were seeing each other. Not only did they "click" on every imaginable level, they had shared interests, passions and goals.

"Mr. Russo's receptionist told me you're still the front-runner for the job."

Niveah whipped around. "She did? When did you talk to her?"

"A few weeks ago."

"Was this before or after…you know."

Jeanette thought for a moment. "I think it was after the Nipplegate incident."

"The Nipplegate incident? What's that?"

"Forget it. I'm not saying another word," she said, shaking

her head. "I don't want to upset you any more than I already have."

"Spit it out," Niveah told her. "I can handle it."

"Okay, but don't say I didn't warn you." After a lengthy pause, she pushed the truth out of her mouth. "The cleaners said you instructed Damien to bite your nipples, and when he did you said, 'That's it, Big Daddy. That's it. That's just the way Mama likes it!'"

The color drained from Niveah's face. Then her legs gave out and she slumped to the floor.

Outside in Tampa's thriving business district, only four blocks away from Access Media and Entertainment, Damien stood in line to buy *The New York Post* at the corner kiosk. He rubbed the sleep from his eyes and patted back a yawn. It had been impossible to wake up this morning. He'd stumbled into the house at dawn and instantly fell into a coma-like sleep. If his housekeeper hadn't dashed cold water on him he'd still be in bed dreaming about Niveah.

Niveah. The witty, engaging woman he'd been spending his days and nights with. Since meeting her he'd forgotten every other girl. Damien didn't want to think any more about their growing relationship, but his thoughts held him hostage. It didn't matter where he was or what he was doing, Niveah Evans was always on his mind.

Damien never imagined that he could meet someone who was perfect for him in every way, but he had. Everything with Niveah was so easy, so natural, so right. Competitive women turned him on, and working side-by-side with her increased his desire. So what was keeping him from popping the question and riding off with Niveah into the sunset? They worked together *and* were vying for the same job. What would happen if he was named vice president in June and she wasn't? Things would go south for sure. And where would that leave him? Nursing a broken heart back in New York, that's where.

The thick, dark clouds floating across the sky threatened heavy rain. Deciding he'd flag down a taxi instead of walking the rest of the way to the office, Damien dug into his jacket, counted out the exact change and handed it to the bearded street vendor.

"Excuse me, young man," a woman trilled behind him. "Can you help us?"

Damien lowered his newspaper and smiled at the petite woman in the aged coat. "Sure, what seems to be the problem?"

A man with a stocky frame and a stern mouth appeared out of nowhere. "We're looking for—" he consulted the piece of paper in his hand "—the Accenture Tower, and we'd be mighty grateful if you could help us."

Frowning, he examined the elderly couple from behind his tinted sunglasses. What business did these people have in his building? With their decades-old clothing and thick, southern accents, they looked like the black version of the *Beverly Hillbillies*. "Why don't we share a cab? I happen to work in that building and I'm headed there now."

"God bless you, young man!" The woman hugged him so tight he couldn't breathe. "We've been wandering around these parts for almost an hour and my legs are about to give way!"

Inside the taxi cab, Damien listened to the couple's tale of woe. The airline had lost their luggage, they'd taken the wrong bus into town and no one would help them.

"By the way, I'm Ida and this here is my husband, Clifford."

"I'm Damien," he said with an easy smile. "What part of the South are you from?"

The woman raised a stenciled eyebrow. "How did you know we were from the south?"

"Your lovely accent gave you away, ma'am."

"Why thank you, son. We came all the way from Chickasaw, Alabama, to visit our daughter. She's expecting us tonight, but since we arrived at the airport six hours early, the ticket agent was nice enough to put us on an earlier flight."

"I bet you can hardly wait to see her."

"Is it that obvious?" Her laugh warmed her entire face. "Norma-Jean flew us down here first class, and even sent us some traveling money. Isn't that special?"

"It sure is." Damien looked out of the window. This woman was a lively free spirit, and being in her company reminded him how much he missed his mom. "I'm sorry you've had such a tough day, but don't sweat it. I grew up here, but I still get lost sometimes!"

The couple laughed along with him.

"What do you do for a living?" The man's eyes slid over his suit, then lingered for several seconds on his watch. "Are you a lawyer or something?"

"No, I'm in the advertising business."

The woman faced him, her light brown eyes wild with excitement. "Just like our daughter! You must know Norma-Jean then. She's tall, with long legs and a big ol' country butt. There's no missing her. She's a real beauty, and I'm not just saying that because she looks like me!"

Damien felt a tickle in his throat, but didn't laugh. "I believe you, ma'am, but no one by that name works at my company."

"Norma-Jean legally changed her name after she left Chickasaw."

The woman's lips twitched and for a moment Damien feared she might cry.

"Why would she do that? I think Norma-Jean is a lovely name."

"I still don't understand it myself. It's like she's ashamed of who she is or something."

The husband picked up where his wife left off. "I keep telling my wife that Norma-Jean meant no harm, but she's taken this thing so personal. Our daughter said to make it in the business world she needed a sophisticated name, and Norma-Jean wouldn't cut it."

"Well, Niveah don't sound no better to me," Ida argued. "Don't sound no better to me at all."

Damien choked on his tongue. His thoughts turned to mush and his heart was hammering so loud in his chest that he couldn't think. He heard what the woman said, but didn't understand. "Are you telling me that Niveah Evans is your daughter?"

"She sure is." The woman smiled from ear to ear. "Do you know her?"

In every sense of the word, Damien thought, picturing Niveah's beautiful naked body. Shaking his head helped to clear the image. He didn't know why, but meeting her parents instantly made him feel closer to her. "Yes, ma'am, I do."

"Isn't she just a peach?"

Damien reexamined the couple, searched their faces for any physical resemblance to Niveah. While she was fair-skinned with fine features her parents were both short, heavy set and shades darker. It was no wonder he didn't realize who they were. "Your daughter is an incredible woman. She lights up every room she enters; and to be honest, I've never met anyone like her."

Mr. Evans wore a crooked grin. "You're sweet on our daughter, aren't you, son?"

"We're here, 1985 Broadway," the taxi driver announced. "You owe me fifteen bucks even."

Damien paid the fare and followed the couple out of the cab. While they waited in the lobby for the elevator, Mrs. Evans fussed with her clothes. "You look very nice, ma'am."

"I just hope Norma-Jean doesn't pass out when she sees us!"

"You and me both," Damien said, looking on as Mrs. Evans tugged at the front of her wig. "I have a feeling this will be a day she'll never forget."

Chapter 14

Niveah winced when Jeanette plopped the ice-pack on top of her head. It felt as if a vise was clamped around her neck, and a sharp, excruciating pain was shooting down her spine. In the hopes of tuning out her best friend, who was hovering over her, fretting, Niveah lowered herself onto the couch and closed her eyes.

"Are you sure you're okay? I don't mind staying here and keeping you company."

"Go, I'm fine." Niveah waved Jeanette away. "I just need to rest for a bit."

"If you're sure…"

"Don't worry I'll be as good as new in an hour."

"I'm check back on you in an hour, okay?"

Niveah waited until she heard the door shut before placing a cushion under her head and stretching out her legs. Water dripped down her face from the ice pack, and splashed onto her blouse like raindrops. *One day I'm on top of the world, the next I'm sprawled flat on my back.*

Crossing her legs at the ankles, she tried to remember everything that had happened before she fainted. Nothing came to mind. It was as if someone had taken a magic eraser to her memory and scrubbed it clean. And what Niveah did remember she desperately wanted to forget. Waking up to find her colleagues gathered around her was humiliating. She wanted to crawl under her desk and die. To reassure her staff that she was okay, she'd sprung to her feet, refused all offers of help and laughed off the whole incident.

Opening one eye, Niveah studied the antique wall clock. Surprised that it was almost ten o'clock, she wondered where Damien was this morning. He was usually here by now, bursting into her office with coffee, pastries and his bright, jovial mood. It was no secret around the office that Damien was a flirt, but when they were together, he made her feel as if no one else mattered. His playfulness brought out the best in her, helped her to relax and not take life so seriously.

The phone on her desk buzzed, but Niveah made no move to answer it. Not when her legs ached and her bones felt as stiff as dried clay. Whoever it was would just have to call back, because right now she was off the clock. Everyone—from the cleaning crew to her boss—knew that she was having an affair with Damien, and until Niveah knew how to handle the situation, she was hiding out in her office.

On the other side of the door, Damien stood in the hallway with Mr. and Mrs. Evans. "You two wait right here. I'm going to go inside and make sure Niveah isn't busy."

"All right, son, but hurry up," Mrs. Evans said, "we're anxious to see our baby girl."

Damien knocked on the door, then popped his head inside Niveah's office. He expected to find her behind her desk, not stretched out on the couch holding an ice pack to her head. "Niveah, what happened? Are you okay?"

Opening her eyes, she snatched the ice pack off her head

and smiled weakly at him. "I fainted, but don't worry, I'm fine. More embarrassed than anything. Thank God Jeanette caught me before I hit the floor, or I would've broken my neck."

Damien lowered himself to the floor. "Is there anything I can get you? Anything you need?"

"No, I'll be all right."

"Well, I have something guaranteed to make you feel better," he said, kissing her forehead.

"You're a sex addict, if I've ever seen one."

"It takes one to know one."

Niveah made a face. "I don't have a problem."

"I beg to differ." Damien brought his mouth to her ear, and a hand to her exposed thigh. He wasn't a fan of business suits, but he loved the feminine cut of Niveah's blazer. The peach color suited her, too. It enhanced the warmth in her eyes and the tone of her skin. "I wasn't the one who initiated sex in the stadium parking lot, or that quickie at the video arcade last week."

At the memory of their sexy late-night encounter, she grinned.

"You know what you are, Niveah? A briefcase freak."

"A what?"

"You're a buttoned-up, briefcase-toting businesswoman who loves sex. And don't try to deny it, because I can see right through you." Damien winked. "Now close your eyes and don't peek."

Moving as stealthily as a cat burglar, he strode over to the door, opened it and waved Mr. and Mrs. Evans inside.

Niveah inhaled deeply. The fragrant scent of cherry blossoms filled the room, instantly conjuring images of her mother working in her prize-winning flower garden. Touched that Damien had bought her flowers the second time this week, she smiled inwardly.

"Surprise!"

At the sound of her mother's voice, Niveah's eyes flew

open. Convinced that the fall she'd suffered earlier had thrown out more than just her back, she blinked until her vision cleared.

Mr. Evans gave his daughter a hug. "We're mighty glad to see you, baby girl." He sniffed, then cleaned his eyes with the sleeve of his plaid shirt. "How have you been keeping?"

In the space of a minute, Niveah went deaf, dumb and blind. Her heart was rattling around her chest, and for a moment all she could do was stare. She sat still, motionless, without moving a muscle. Standing beside Damien, dressed in the same clothes they'd worn to her university graduation a decade earlier, were her parents, Ida and Clifford Evans. Her mother's skin was wrinkled with age and her father was rounder across the middle, but they both looked strong and healthy.

Feelings of shock and confusion engulfed her. What were her parents doing here—Niveah swallowed the lump of fear wedged inside her throat—twelve hours ahead of schedule? And more importantly, what were they doing with Damien?

A fresh wave of panic caused her body to shake. Had her mom told him where they were from? *Of course she did. No one's prouder to be from Chickasaw than Ida Evans!* "Welcome to Tampa." It was a lame greeting, devoid of emotion, but seeing her parents had left her tongue-tied. "How was your flight? Everything went okay?"

"The airline lost our luggage, but they promised to deliver it to your house once they sort everything out. Aside from that, the trip was great."

Niveah shot Damien a *what is going on?* look, but instead of responding he grinned like the lovable mischief-maker he was.

"Come over here and give me some suga'," Mrs. Evans said, holding out her fleshy arms. Before Niveah could move, her mom rushed forward and embraced her.

To keep from toppling over, Niveah grabbed the front of

the bookshelf. A laugh burst out of her mouth. Her mother hadn't changed one bit. She was still as lively as ever.

"Well, aren't you a tall glass of cold water." Mrs. Evans shook her head as she spoke, disapproval on her face and in her tone. "Norma-Jean, you're nothing but skin and bones. I'm going to have to fatten you up real nice while I'm here."

Mr. Evans whistled as he glanced around her office. "This is a mighty fine setup you've got here, baby girl. Looks like your company is taking good care of you." Walking farther into the room, he pointed at the plaques, framed magazine covers and awards prominently displayed on the walls and shelves. "Do these all belong to you, baby girl?"

Niveah nodded.

Her mother gave a shout of joy. "Imagine that, our daughter, the first African-American vice president of this big-time advertising agency!"

"Hold your horses, Mom. I don't have the job yet."

Her parents laughed.

"I don't mean to interrupt, but I have a meeting with the boss in fifteen minutes. It's been a pleasure meeting you, Mr. and Mrs. Evans, and I hope that you enjoy your stay in Tampa."

Damien had been so quiet Niveah forgot that he was in the room.

"Thanks again for all your help, son." Mr. Evans shook Damien's hand, then turned back to his daughter. "If not for this young man's help, your mother and I would still be wandering around downtown looking for your office."

"We'd love to have you over one night for dinner, son. You know, to show our appreciation. You like barbeque chicken wings and black-eyed peas?"

"I sure do!" His eyes were wide, alert, as if he'd just guzzled down an energy drink. "You just let me know when, and I'll be there!"

Mrs. Evans giggled like a teenage girl high on sugar. "All right, then it's a date."

"I can hardly wait." He smacked his lips, which drew laughs from everyone in the room. "Nothing beats down-home cooking, and it's been a long time since I've eaten Southern food."

Scared her mother would launch into a detailed rundown of her best recipes, Niveah made a beeline for the door. "If it's okay with you guys, I'm going to walk Damien to his office."

"Take your time." Her mother gave a dismissive wave. "Don't rush on account of us."

"Do you need anything? I can ask my assistant to bring you something if you're hungry."

Her dad shook his head. "We ate plenty on the plane. We're fine. Now, go on."

Damien opened the door and Niveah stepped past him out into the hall.

"I really appreciate you helping my parents out this morning," Niveah said, raising her voice to be heard about the flurry of excitement in the department. "It was very kind of you."

"Your mom and dad are my kind of people. Friendly, outgoing, funny as hell. You must have had a really great childhood."

Niveah felt his eyes on her, watching her, but she didn't dare look at him. Discussing her childhood was off limits. It didn't matter that she trusted Damien and enjoyed spending time with him; there were some things better left in the past, and her formative years in Chickasaw was one of them. "Do you mind briefing Mr. Russo on the S.W.A.G. ad campaign? I'm going to take my parents back to my place, but I'll be back within—"

Damien grabbed Niveah around the waist, ducked inside the storage room and slammed the door with his foot. "I'm dying to see what you've got on under this suit." His voice was unbearably husky. He dropped his suitcase on the floor and flashed a dirty little grin. "I need this, baby. I need you."

"In light of what I found out this morning, making out in here is the last thing we should be—" Her protest died on her lips when he kissed her. All thought and reason disappeared. Vanished. Floated away like a balloon in the sky.

Instinctively, Niveah moved closer and coiled her arms around his neck. A sigh slipped from between her lips. Enjoying the sexual chemistry pulsing between them, she kissed him deeply, passionately, with everything she had.

Rocking her hips against his groin created the most delicious friction. Her lips deserted his mouth to nibble, nip and tease his earlobe. Niveah ran her hands along his jaw, down his shoulders and across his chest. Leaning into him, so close that she could feel his heart beating through his shirt, she tried valiantly to suppress her raging sexual hunger. But surrendering to her passions was thrilling, exhilarating, the single most freeing thing she'd ever done.

The door handle rattled, scaring Niveah straight. Ending the kiss, she stepped back and listened intently for several nerve racking seconds. Her stomach clenched and knotted, knotted and clenched. Holding her breath, she prayed that the disgruntled intern grumbling outside the storage room door would return to her office. Niveah sighed in relief when she heard the distant sound of footsteps.

"That was close." Damien wiped imaginary sweat from his brow. "Now where were we?"

"I'm getting out of here. I'll see you in an hour."

"No one's getting in here. The door's locked, and besides, it's almost break time. In ten minutes the office will be deserted."

"Damien, everyone knows."

"Knows what?"

"That we're lovers." Niveah told him everything. About

the nosy cleaners, the snitch in the marketing department and that word had reached their boss. "I've never been so humiliated."

"Is that why you fainted?"

Niveah stared out the window so he wouldn't see the truth on her face. "It doesn't matter. I exercised poor judgment last Sunday in your office, and now I'm the laughingstock of the entire company. Do you have any idea how that makes me feel?"

"That's what you get for making all that noise," he teased. "I told you to keep it down."

"How was I supposed to know the cleaners were outside in the hall listening? And furthermore, I wouldn't have squealed if you hadn't dribbled chocolate syrup down my back."

"Baby, you're right. It's my fault. Next time I promise to heat it up for you."

"Damien, there won't be a next time. Didn't you hear what I just said? Everyone knows that we're lovers," she repeated, edging away, out of his reach. "That includes management, the creative department team and my staff."

"Who cares?"

"I do!" Niveah threw her hands up in the air. "Don't you get it? Our relationship could jeopardize my chances of being named company VP."

"The executive committee will base their decision on merit, not on a candidate's personal life. What we do after hours is no one's business but our own."

Incredulous and aggravated that he was downplaying the gravity of the situation, she shook her head. "You know what, Damien? The last few weeks have been fun, but it's time for me to refocus my energy on work. I have more projects than I know what to do with, and the higher-ups are depending on me to woo these new international clients."

"Are you sure this is what you want?"

"I'm positive." Niveah reached for the door handle.

"Nothing is more important to you than being named vice president, huh?"

"That's all that matters."

The silence seemed to last forever.

"I shouldn't be surprised," he conceded, his tone brisk and matter-of-fact, "considering you changed your entire identity to advance your career."

"You don't know anything about me."

"I know you changed your name, haven't been back to Chickasaw since you graduated from college and are embarrassed about where you come from."

The truth was a large, painful knot in her chest.

"You had no right to grill my parents about me."

"Is that what you think I did?" The look on his face could scare a serial killer. "Your parents couldn't stop bragging about their big shot daughter who works in advertising, and over the course of our conversation I realized that they were referring to you. Naturally, I was confused when they called you Norma-Jean, and asked. Did you ever consider how your mother would feel about you disowning her great-grandmother's name?"

His question hung in the air like an invisible cloud of smoke. It was so quiet in the storage room that Niveah could hear the photocopier printing across the hall.

"Changing your name hurt your mom deeply."

"She told you that?"

"She didn't have to. I saw the pain in her eyes."

Niveah's stomach ached violently, and she could hardly breathe.

"You know, things don't have to be this way."

"I'm afraid they do. We both knew what this was from day one, so don't pretend to be heartbroken that it's over." To fight the sudden wave of emotion that washed over her, she made light of the situation. "Don't worry, Damien, I'm sure you'll find another *briefcase freak* before the day's over. In a couple days I'll be a distant memory. Just another woman you—"

"Shut up and listen." His tone was harsh, but is his eyes were filled with concern. "I don't want to talk about this in here, but what I have to say to you can't wait."

Blinking rapidly, she stared at him, confused. Damien looked troubled, as if there were a war waging in his mind. He smoothed a hand over his goatee, mumbled a few words she didn't understand then blew out a deep, ragged breath.

"I can deliver a speech in front of the richest businessmen in the world, but I can't tell the woman I love how I feel. Go figure."

Niveah couldn't speak. Her tongue suddenly felt too big for her mouth, and she feared what would come out if she tried to talk.

"Because of what happened with my ex, I refused to let anyone get too close. I was content playing the field, moving from one girl to the next. Settling down with one woman and having a family was never part of the plan, but then I met you, and my life hasn't been the same since."

Smiling sadly, he reached out and drew his thumb over her cheek.

"I thought it was the sex that kept me coming back for more, but last night as I watched you sleep, I realized that sex has nothing to do with it. I don't love just one thing about you, Niveah, I love everything. Your intelligence, your confidence and your poise."

Her anger began to fade, and the more he spoke the more her eyes burned with tears.

"I don't care what your birth name is, where you come from or if you had buckteeth as a child. All I care about is being with you for the rest of my life."

Niveah wrung her hands fitfully behind her back. She was never going to be rid of her fears and insecurities, and she couldn't risk Damien finding out the truth—that she was a scared, insecure woman who suffered from low self-esteem. How many times over the years had she been told she wasn't beautiful enough? Was stiff and boring in bed? Excelling in the advertising world was easy, but having a successful relationship had eluded her for years. And Damien's confession, though heartfelt and sincere, would never change that.

"I-I'm touched by what you just said, but..." Niveah ignored the pleading look in his eyes and lied with the conviction of a thief caught in the act of stealing. "I need to stay focused on my upcoming projects. I have a million-dollar campaign to wrap up, two companies that are expecting a proposal for their products next week, and a launch party for S.W.A.G. to plan."

"In other words, discussing our relationship is a waste of your valuable time."

"Your words, not mine."

Stunned by how selfish she could be, Damien tried to control the anger pulsing through his veins. He studied her closely, saw her rigid posture and narrowed eyes. Her wall was back up—her shield of protective armor designed to keep him and everyone else who cared about her at bay. Damien wanted to grab her, shake some sense in her, but doubted that would help.

"I guess I'll be seeing you."

It was with a heavy heart Damien watched Niveah leave. She was gone, out of his life forever, and the realization was more painful than a stake to the heart.

Chapter 15

Spending the afternoon fighting through thick crowds wasn't Niveah's idea of a good time, but since her parents wanted to check out Gospel Fest at Fairfield Park, she'd donned a wide-brimmed hat and driven the thirty miles to the outdoor venue.

"Good Lord, it's packed out here, and hot, too," her mother complained as they ambled into the park. "I want to sit right in front of the stage."

Stunned by the staggering number of families, teens and couples in attendance, Niveah searched for a vacant spot on the field. Clowns painted faces, vendors sold ice cream and the audience sang along with the singers onstage. A light breeze was blowing, but it did nothing to curtail the intensity of the sun. "We should set up under the trees. It's expected to reach ninety-five degrees, and we're going to need the shade."

"Good point, baby girl." Mr. Evans cleaned the sweat from his forehead with his trusty, white handkerchief. "This festival puts the spring fair in Chickasaw to shame. I reckon there are two, three thousand people here."

Her mother wiggled her hips to the beat of the music. "I'm really glad Damien suggested this event. He was right, the performers are talented and the atmosphere is festive and lively."

So *that's* how her parents knew about Gospel Fest. Niveah wondered if Damien had also recommended the guided walking tour through downtown, that little out-of-the-way Creole restaurant, and the weekend dinner cruise.

"We need to find a spot soon," her mother said. "I'm tired of holding these darn chairs."

Five minutes later, they settled down on the east side of the field. While her dad set up the folding table, her mom busied herself with unpacking the cooler.

"I can't get over how good these bands are." Humming, she picked up a knife and sliced her roast beef sandwich in half. "Clifford, what do you think about having live music at our anniversary dinner? That would certainly liven things up, don't you think?"

"That's a good idea, Ida, but I don't know the first thing about booking a band." Mr. Evans turned to his daughter. "Baby girl, I know you're really busy at work, but do you think you could come home a few weeks before the party and help me scout out some entertainment?"

Niveah had been waiting for the right time to talk to her parents about their anniversary party, and although this wasn't the venue she would have chosen, now seemed as good a time as any. "I won't be able to attend the party."

Her father's jaw dropped and her mother gasped.

"What do you mean you won't be able to make it?" they asked in unison.

"I have an advertising conference to attend in Vermont that weekend."

Mrs. Evans chucked her plate down on the table. "But it's

our fortieth wedding anniversary! Isn't that more important than some silly work function?"

"Mom, we can celebrate before you leave next Sunday. We can go anywhere you want."

"You're our only daughter, our only child, and we want to share this special time with you and the rest of the family," Mr. Evans explained, his cap in his hand. "I've never begged anyone for anything in my life, but I'm begging you, Norma-Jean. Please reconsider coming home."

Niveah stared at her dad, shocked by what she saw. Were those tears in his eyes? He spoke in a broken, jagged whisper, as if talking was causing him physical pain. But at the thought of returning to Chickasaw, to the place where she'd been ridiculed, teased and bullied for eighteen years, her heart raced out of control.

"Don't do it for me," her father continued. "Do it for your mom. It would mean the world to her to have you there."

"I'm sorry we couldn't…" Her mother sniffed, tried to finish, then shook her head as if she was too distressed to speak.

"We know you hated growing up in Chickasaw, and we're sorry we couldn't provide for you better, but times were tough in the late sixties, and—"

Niveah cut him off. "Dad, what are you talking about? You and Mom were great parents. The best. I couldn't have asked for anything more."

"Do you really mean that, Norma-Jean?" Her mom blotted her damp cheeks with a napkin. "You don't resent us for not taking better care of you?"

"Mom, I'm deeply grateful for all the sacrifices you made for me. You're the reason I am who I am today, and I owe all of my success to you." Niveah leaned over and hugged her parents. "I love you both, and I'm going to miss you when you leave next week."

"That's all the more reason for you to come home."

"I'll try my best."

Her mom cheered. "This is the best news ever! Wait until I tell everyone!"

"I told your mother you wouldn't let us down," her father said, patting her leg. "And I'm real glad we made the trip down here. I see why you like living in Tampa. It's a real nice city, doesn't seem dangerous at all."

Niveah laughed and looked on as her parents stood up and danced along with the lively, fifty-person youth choir on stage. Her thoughts drifted to Damien, to the man who had come to mean so much to her in the last four months. Up until last week, she never would have guessed that he'd want to be in a committed relationship, but that's exactly what he'd offered her in the office storage room. And what had she done? Blown him off.

"Would you two mind being interviewed on camera?"

Niveah turned around. Out of nowhere, an Asian woman with a camera crew had appeared.

"Oh, sure," Mrs. Evans said, fluffing her hair. "My sister's going to be jealous when she sees this!"

Five minutes of setup, and the reporter was ready to go. "Good afternoon. This is Hannah Chan for WJAC-TV reporting live from Gospel Fest 2010. Standing beside me are Ida and Clifford Evans from Chickasaw, Alabama. Are you two enjoying yourself this afternoon?"

"We sure are," Mrs. Evans said, snatching the microphone out of the reporter's hand. "Tampa's a real fine city, and everyone we've met has been just delightful. This is our first time here, but it certainly won't be our last. Our daughter, Norma-Jean, is…"

Niveah's cell phone rang, drawing her attention away from her parent's interview. The number that appeared on the screen was vaguely familiar, but she couldn't remember who it belonged to. Guessing it was a client, she said, "Hello, Ms. Niveah Evans speaking."

"Your mom's a natural," Damien said, his voice loud and clear. "That reporter better watch out before Mama Evans steals her job!"

At the sound of his hearty chuckle, Niveah laughed, too. Worried she'd be picked up on camera, she stood and walked across the field. "Don't tell me you're watching this?"

"I sure am. Your parents are incredibly entertaining, and I love their matching 'I Love Tampa' T-shirts."

"I'll tell them you approve. By the way, thanks for recommending Gospel Fest. As you can see they're having the time of their lives."

A long, awkward silence followed.

"You look *real* good, Niveah."

"What are you talking about? You can't see me through the phone."

"I don't need to see you to know you look gorgeous, but I did spot you when the cameraman panned the crowd. You're hard to miss in that enormous hat and pretty little dress."

Niveah glanced around, half expecting him to pop out from behind the bushes.

"When am I going to see you?"

"I saw you yesterday."

"That doesn't count. We were in a budget meeting with thirty-five other people," he pointed out. "Can we meet somewhere tonight to talk?"

"Damien, I can't."

"We're only going to talk. You have my word. Nothing more is going to happen."

Niveah couldn't stop herself from teasing him. "I've heard *that* before. You better be careful, Mr. Hunter. You're beginning to sound like a broken record."

"I blame you. You've got my mind twisted, and now I'm trippin' big time." His laugh was easy. "I'd be tossed out of Delta Phi on my ass, if my fraternity brothers heard me now!"

Niveah tightened her grip on her cell phone, but kept her voice level, calm. "We're not seeing each other romantically anymore, and I think meeting up tonight is a bad idea."

"Well, I don't, so tuck your parents in and meet me at the Ritz-Carlton for drinks. Is ten o'clock too late?"

"You're not suggesting I sneak out of the house, are you?"

"Damn right I am!" He chuckled. "Please, Niveah? I'm heading back to New York on Monday, and it would mean a lot if I could see you before I leave."

"You're taking another trip back east? Is it for business or pleasure?"

"I'll tell you all about it when we meet up later tonight."

The excitement of seeing him overrode her good sense, and before Niveah could second-guess her decision, she agreed. "Okay, I'll meet you, but only for an hour."

"That's all I need," he said, quickly. "Oh, and one more thing, wear that outfit you had on at the S.W.A.G. photo shoot last month."

"Why?"

"Because I can't get the image of you in that dress out of my mind."

Niveah's heart fluttered, but it was the silky hue of his voice and the subtle, sexual undertones of his words that told her talking about the demise of their relationship was the last thing on Damien's mind.

Niveah pushed open the back door and shuffled into the kitchen. Forcing a smile on her lips, she dumped her leather briefcase on the tile floor and greeted her mom. "It smells good in here, Mom. What are you making?"

"Okra gumbo with cornmeal dumplings."

Niveah wrinkled her nose. "I think I'll just have a salad. I'm really not that hungry."

"But you used to love my gumbo. It was your favorite food growing up."

That's because there was nothing else to eat. Painful memories from the past resurfaced. As a child, she'd watched her mother water down soup, scrounge through garbage bins for discarded bottles and stand in long lines at government agencies. There was never enough money, never enough food. Her colleagues didn't understand why she worked around the clock, but Niveah didn't expect them to. They'd never had to eat at homeless shelters, or wear second-hand clothes. The first taste of success had encouraged her to work harder, and now she was just weeks away from achieving her ultimate goal of buying her parents their dream home.

"I stopped eating that a long time ago, but you and Dad go ahead. I'll find something else to eat." Niveah plopped onto a chair. "Mom, you weren't even supposed to cook today. I told you yesterday we were going out for dinner."

"I appreciate the offer, baby girl, but I'm tired of eating out."

"But we've only eaten out twice since you got here."

"Exactly!" He mother nodded her head vigorously. "All your father and I want to do tonight is spend a quiet evening at home with you."

"Okay, you won't get an argument out of me. I'm exhausted."

"Of course you are! It's six-thirty and you're just getting home. I can't believe you keep such peculiar work hours."

"There's my baby girl."

At the sound of her father's voice, Niveah turned around in her chair. The smile on her lips froze at the sight of Damien standing beside her dad. Her heart melted in a puddle at her feet. His cologne drifted into the room, blending smoothly with the tangy aromas in the air.

"We thought you'd never get home," Damien said, leaning

casually against the wall. "How was work? I phoned you around lunchtime, but the call went straight to voicemail."

"I was meeting with a client."

Mr. Evans gave his daughter a peck on the cheek and then hustled over to the stove. "I sure hope dinner's ready. I haven't eaten anything since we returned from fishing, and I'm starvin'!"

"You went fishing? Where? With who?"

"Damien took your father out this afternoon," her mother explained. "Isn't that nice?"

Niveah rolled her eyes so hard her temples throbbed. "Yeah, he's as charitable as they come."

"Honey, will you be a dear and set the patio table?" Mrs. Evans pointed at the plates and cutlery on the center island. "Everything you need is right there, and don't forget to wipe the table down. It looks sticky."

"I'll help." Whistling a tune, Damien grabbed the placemats and followed Niveah through the sliding glass doors. "It looks like a storm's brewing out here. I sure hope it doesn't rain."

The sky was dark and overcast, which mirrored Niveah's foul mood. She'd had a horrible day, and for some reason, seeing Damien here, all up in her personal space, annoyed her.

"You look worn out. Are you okay?"

"I'm fine. Just peachy." The plates made a clattering sound when Niveah dropped them on the table. To prevent her parents from eavesdropping, she closed the door and came around the table. "Damien, what are you doing here?"

"Hanging out with Ma and Pa Evans, of course." He chuckled, then sported a grin that lit up his eyes. "I returned from New York this afternoon and called to see how you guys were doing. Your father mentioned wanting to go to Fort Desoto to fish, so I offered to take him. When I dropped him off, your mom insisted I stay for dinner. Is that a problem?"

"I know my parents are amusing to you, but I won't have you laughing at my expense."

"Why is it so hard for you to believe that I like spending time with your parents? They're great people, and they remind me a lot of my mom and dad." The set of his chin, and the raw emotion in his tone spoke to his anger. "Your parents and I had a long talk this afternoon, but despite everything they told me about your upbringing, I still don't understand why you push yourself to the point of exhaustion."

"Because when I was a kid I had everything against me!" she shouted, pointing a finger at her chest. "You don't know what it's like to go without, Damien. I do. I've built a successful life for myself and I'm damn proud of it. And I won't let you or anyone else stand in the way of me achieving my goals."

"You're going to show everyone back in Chickasaw that you're somebody. That you're smart and talented and accomplished. That's what drives you, what motivates you, isn't it?"

"Why do you make it sound like such a bad thing?"

"Because it's at the expense of two people who love you very much."

"This isn't about my parents."

Damien grunted. "That's where you're wrong, Niveah. When you turned your back on Chickasaw, you turned your back on them. At least that's the way they see it."

Offended by what he was implying, she lashed back. "You're *way* off base, and I'll have you know that I take great care of my mom and dad. I send them money, cover the cost of their home repairs and have a considerable retirement fund saved up for them."

"Niveah, your parents appreciate everything you've done for them, but you know what would make them happier than anything in the world? Seeing you more than once every five years. I know this is none of my business, and that I've already said enough, but, Niveah, it's important that you attend their anniversary party. They want you there to celebrate with their friends and family."

"I—I can't. You don't know what it was like growing up there. It was horrible, and just the thought of returning to Chickasaw makes me sick to my stomach."

"You don't have to go alone. I'll go with you."

"I couldn't ask you to do that."

"You're not. I'm offering." His voice was soft, filled with warmth and concern. "Niveah, needing someone doesn't make you weak. It makes you human."

Her breath caught when he touched her arm. "Damien, you…you shouldn't be here."

"After what happened last Saturday, I thought you'd be happy to see me."

Niveah didn't dare look Damien in the eye. This was all her fault. Instead of meeting Damien at the Ritz-Carlton to talk, they'd ended up in suite 12—the very suite they'd made love in on New Year's Eve. But this time there was wine, music and a late-night meal that whet her palate. Sleeping with Damien had been the furthest thing from Niveah's mind, but when he kissed her she melted into his arms. He'd held her close, whispered in her ear, told her she was the woman he'd been searching for his entire life. In his arms, she felt adored, cherished—everything Damien said she was and more. Making love to him that night had proved that they didn't have to be swinging from the chandeliers to have great sex. Their lovemaking had been sweet, filled with tender, heartfelt moments, and the most satisfying sexual experience of Niveah's life.

"I owe you an apology," she began, searching for the right words. "I've been sending you mixed signals. Damien, you're a great guy, but I'm not interested in a serious relationship. I just don't have the time."

"You're lying."

"No one turns you down, is that it?" Her tone was filled with anger. "You're a walking cliché. The typical high-powered businessman who's so used to having his way with women, he can't handle being rejected."

"I used to be just like you—working around the clock, chasing the almighty dollar, putting clients above all else. Promotions and material possessions used to mean the world to me, and then I got the worst possible news ever and my life changed in an instant. A year ago…" Damien stumbled over his words, then coughed, and tried again. "My dad was—"

Her cell phone rang drowning out the rest of his sentence. Smiling apologetically, Niveah retrieved it from her jacket pocket and flipped it open. When she saw the phone number on the screen her shoulders drooped. "Hello." She sighed deeply, an exasperated look on her face. "Sure, no problem, sir, I'm on my way."

"What's up?" Damien asked when she slapped her phone shut. "Is everything okay?"

"Mr. Russo wants me back at the office. The representatives from the big food company hate the ad campaign and are threatening to find another agency if we don't fix it tonight."

"Niveah, I don't understand why you insist on doing everyone else's job. If there's a problem with the proposal, Mr. Russo should call the account manager or someone in client services. It's their job to sell the client on the brief, not you."

"I know, but as creative director it ultimately falls on my shoulders," she explained, her voice tense. "Most of our clients have to be handled with kid gloves. You know that."

"So you're going to blow off dinner with your family just because Mr. Russo called?"

"This is my job, Damien. They'll understand."

He shook his head, his face covered in surprise and

disappointment. "It's amazing that someone who mentors teens, and *claims* to love her family, could be so selfish."

Inside Niveah a storm was brewing. She was so angry her entire body was shaking. Narrowing her eyes, she stepped forward and fixed her hands rigidly on her hips. "I don't understand why you're taking this so personally, Damien. It doesn't concern you. It's my life, and I can do whatever the hell I want."

"You know what? I was wrong. You are the perfect woman for the VP job. The higher-ups are looking for someone who'll forsake their life for the company, and they've found a real winner in you." His laugh was tinged with disgust. "And to think I was planning to propose to you. That would have been pretty stupid, huh? I thought if I showed you how special you are to me, you'd make room for me in your life. But it was foolish of me to think that way. Nothing I ever say or do will change who you are, and I just have to accept that."

Tears formed in Niveah's eyes. They hurt, pierced, stung almost as much as his words. Niveah couldn't breathe, couldn't move, couldn't talk. Not that she had anything to say. She tried to fight the feelings that overwhelmed her, but she suddenly had no control over her emotions. "I—I—I never knew you felt that way."

"Would it have made any difference?"

The patio door slid open. Mr. Evans appeared, balancing a casserole dish in his hands that carried a spicy, mouth-watering aroma. "I hope ya'll are done talking, because we're hungry. Mom's on the phone with Grandma Cicely, but she'll be out shortly."

Niveah turned away so her dad wouldn't see her tear-stained face.

"I'm afraid I have to go," Damien said. "Please extend my deepest apologies to your wife."

"Sure, son. Would you like to take a plate home?"

"No, thank you." Damien shook Mr. Evans's hand. His

smile was thin, forced, as fake as a department store Santa. "If I don't see you before you leave, have a safe trip."

"It was a pleasure meeting you, son. Take good care of yourself, and my daughter."

"That won't be necessary, sir. I think she's got that covered." Then, without so much as a glance in Niveah's direction, he jogged down the steps and strode out of the backyard.

Chapter 16

"Call me as soon as you get home," Niveah ordered, her voice stern. "I don't care how late it is."

"We will, baby girl, and thanks for everything. We had a swell time."

"Are you guys sure you can't stay a few more days?" Thankful her sunglasses concealed the tears in her eyes, she slipped a hand around her father's waist and rested her head on his chest. "I can take the week off work and we can drive down to Miami. You've always wanted to see the Miami Dolphins play, Dad. This is your big chance."

Mr. Evans shook his head. "I wish we could stay longer, but Grandma Cicely isn't doing too well, and there's no one around to take care of her."

"I understand, and give Grandma a big kiss for me when you see her." Opening her purse, she retrieved a white envelope and handed it to her dad. "This is for you. I wanted you to have this just in case I don't make it to your anniversary party."

He stepped back and stared at the envelope as if it was laced in anthrax.

"We'll accept it on June twenty-ninth and not a second sooner." Mrs. Evans snatched the card and shoved it into the bottom of her daughter's purse. "We'll see you in three weeks time, and don't forget to bring Damien."

"Mom, we're colleagues. Nothing more. I've told you that a hundred times. Why don't you believe me?"

"Fiddlesticks. I might be old, but I'm not dead. I've been around the block a few times, and I know true love when I see it," she quipped, with a fervent nod of her head. "Your father and I don't want to hear you had a quick shotgun wedding, so bring Damien home so he can meet the rest of the family, ya hear? Now go back over to the ticket booth and book your flight before all the seats are taken."

Niveah laughed. "Right, like Alabama's a hot tourist destination."

"I know. That's why you need to hurry and make your travel arrangements!"

"This is the final boarding call for flight 1752, with stops in Houston and…"

Mr. Evans grabbed his carry-on bag. "Ida, honey, that's us. We better hustle."

Another round of hugs and they were gone. Niveah watched her parents walk through the departure gates and waved when her mom blew her a kiss. They were swallowed up in the sea of travelers and within seconds faded out of sight.

Long after they were gone, Niveah remained in terminal One. For the first time since leaving Chickasaw, she felt utterly and completely alone. The thought of returning to an empty house was depressing, and going to the office held even less appeal.

To perk herself up, she grabbed a coffee and a cinnamon roll and slowly made her way through the airport. Ten minutes later, Niveah paid her parking fee and got behind the wheel of her car. She was pulling out of the underground garage when her cell phone rang.

"Hey, girl. What's up? Are you still at the airport?"

"No, I'm just leaving. How's work?"

"It's the same ol' same ol' around here. Mr. Russo's on a tear because someone in design screwed up on the men's shaving ad. I can't wait for that old man to retire. He's driving everyone crazy!" Jeanette complained. "Anyways, Roxi and I are going to the five o'clock yoga class and I thought you might want to come."

Niveah peered around the car in front of her. Traffic was bumper-to-bumper, crawling painfully slow down Airport Road. Going to the office was out of the question, but she didn't feel like doing the Downward-Facing Dog either. "No, thanks. One yoga class a year is more than enough for me."

"All right. It's your loss!"

"Have you seen Damien around today?"

"Nope, he called in sick again," she reported. "He's been out almost a week. I hope everything's okay."

You and me both. No one knew why he wasn't at work, but everyone was concerned. He'd made an immediate impact on the department from the beginning, and without him there to crack jokes and lighten the mood, the workday seemed to drag on.

"Have you tried calling him?"

The question caught Niveah napping. She started to lie, then said, "Yes, but he's not answering any of his numbers."

"Then go by his place."

"I thought of that, but…"

"But what? What if he's really sick or had a bad accident? Wouldn't you want to know?"

"Of course I would! It's just that I was the one to break things off. I suggested a clean break. No dates, no calls and no text messages. How will it look now if I go back on what I said?"

"Who cares how it looks? Your man has been MIA for days and you need to do what any good girlfriend would do. Find out what's going on."

"That's just it. I'm not his girlfriend. We were…lovers. That's all."

"Casual lovers, huh?" A beat, then, "Niveah, I know you were devastated when Stewart called off the wedding, but don't let that hold you back from committing to Damien. You guys bring out the best in each other, and it's obvious to everyone around here that he loves you. Take a chance, girl. You're a good woman and you deserve to find your prince charming."

Niveah gave some thought to what her friend said. There were so many things about Damien she loved, so many things about him she admired. He was patient with her, always there when she needed him and would do anything to make her happy. Damien filled her life with such joy—corny, yes—but true. But was he telling the truth about loving her? Model types fell at his feet practically every day. Why would he want to be with her?

"Go check on your man and ring me later. We're going to the Ocean Bistro after our yoga class, so when you're done doing—" she giggled, cleared her throat, then continued "—I mean, *talking* to Damien, just meet us there."

"Jeanette, I can't just show up at his house unannounced."

"Why not? Girl, I swear, sometimes I don't get you. You miss him, but you're acting like you don't. That makes no sense to me."

"Who said anything about missing him?" she lied. "I just want to make sure he's okay. I'd do the same if someone else on the creative team had just up and disappeared."

"Puh-leese. You've got it bad for him. That's why you've been so crotchety the last few days. Everybody thinks so. Sure, you say you're stressed out about the S.W.A.G. launch, but I know what's really going on. You're experiencing sexual withdrawal. I read about it just yesterday in *Women's Health* magazine..."

As Niveah listened to Jeanette's psycho babble, she remembered something. Reaching into the backseat, she groped around on the floor for her briefcase. The S.W.A.G. file was still tucked neatly in the side pocket. Damien still hadn't signed off on the calendar, and without his approval she couldn't proceed. Now, only one problem remained. "I couldn't go see Damien even if I wanted to. I don't know where he lives."

Jeanette's voice warmed. "Well, this must be your lucky day, because I have his home address right here."

To be sure she was at the right place, Niveah grabbed the candy bar wrapper she'd jotted Damien's address on and scrutinized it. "Eighteen twenty-six Westshore Boulevard," she read, glancing out the windshield at the attractive single-family home. "This is it."

Niveah gripped the door handle but didn't open it. *What am I waiting for? Courage,* said the voice inside her head. Coming to see Damien seemed like a good idea an hour ago, but now fear churned in her stomach. What if he blew up at her? Or kicked her out? After all, they'd been seeing each other for months and he'd never once invited her to his place. And this was just the kind of thing men were always accusing women of: overstepping their bounds.

Niveah blew out a breath and ran a hand through her hair. She could do this. All she had to do was walk up to the door and ring the bell. It was as simple as that. *So why am I still sitting here gazing up at the house?*

Before she lost her nerve, she unbuckled her seat belt and unlocked the door. That's as far as Niveah got. All eyes, she watched as a female in a black, late model Mustang turned into the driveway. With her cell phone wedged between her ear and her shoulder, the buxom Spanish girl unloaded grocery bags from the trunk and hurried up the walkway. On her way inside, she paused to grab the letters from the mailbox.

Niveah leapt out of the car as if it were on fire. Leaving was definitely out of the question now. Not until she found out who had just sashayed into Damien's house. Moving faster than a professional speed walker, she dashed across the street and flew up the decorative stone steps.

Niveah jabbed the doorbell and didn't stop until she saw a silhouette through the mosaic glass door. It opened and there she was. The mystery woman with the dark hair and taut curves. She was even prettier up close. Clear skin. Big boobs. Most likely real.

"Hello, how can I help you?"

Niveah instantly recognized her voice. It was the same woman who'd picked up Damien's home phone a few months ago. "Are you Mrs. Damien Hunter?"

"I wish." She giggled, and popped her gum. "I'm Marietta. How can I help you?"

"Where's Damien?"

"In the backyard. Who should I say is calling—"

Niveah spun around, and hustled around to the side of the house before the woman could stop her. The backyard had tons of green space, a cluster of towering trees and a large shed beside the garage. Damien was shoveling sand into a small manmade pond. Shirtless, wearing nothing but white basketball shorts, it was impossible not to admire his lean physique. Her eyes crawled down his sweat-slick chest. *Damn, he was fine.* Hands down, the best-looking man she had ever dated. His body, all muscles, abs and pecs, could make a nun weak. Hence the reason why she wanted to slap him *and* kiss him at the same time.

To regain control, Niveah forced all thoughts of sexing Damien to the furthest corner of her mind. They had a profound attraction, one she'd just have to find a way to ignore while she cursed him out. Her sandals pounded on the cement as she strode around the corner, and with each step her anger grew. Damien was a no-good, mangy-dog and when she was done with him he wouldn't know up from down.

"Marietta, could you be a dear and bring me a glass of water?"

"Sorry, wrong girl." Niveah expected Damien to be surprised, but when he turned around he was wearing an amused expression on his face. Then he had the nerve to smile as if he'd just been handed a check for a million dollars from Publisher's Clearing House. "Your girlfriend told me I could find you out here. I hope I'm not interrupting anything."

As if on cue, the back door swung open and the woman of the house appeared. "Damien, I'm sorry. I tried to stop her, but she took off before I could…"

"Don't sweat it, Marietta. It's cool."

"If you need me, I'll be inside preparing lunch."

"You certainly like them young," Niveah said when the girl left. "Is she even twenty?"

"Actually, Marietta's twenty-six." Damien stuck his shovel in the dirt and propped his arms on top of the metal handle. "I'd ask to what do I owe this pleasure, but I have a feeling this conversation is going to be anything but pleasurable."

"I'm here because I need you to sign off on the proofs for the S.W.A.G. calendar." Because of his absence, she'd been burning the candle at both ends all week; and seeing the calm, unperturbed expression on his face pissed her off. To stick it to him, she gestured with her head to the back door and said, "While you've been busy playing house, I've been busting my ass getting ready for the S.W.A.G. launch."

Damien took off his gloves and cleaned his hands on his shorts. "Hand over the proofs. I'll look at them now, so you can be on your way."

Niveah's entire body flushed with embarrassment. In her haste to play investigative reporter, she'd forgotten the folder in her car. But she couldn't tell Damien that, so she asked the question dangling off the tip of her tongue. "How many of us are there?"

"Us?" He walked over to the porch, retrieved the white shirt on the steps and shrugged it on. "You're going to have to explain, because don't know what the hell you're talking about."

"You think you're slick, don't you? Running game on lonely, single women who'll do anything to be with someone as successful as you." Niveah knew that her voice teetered on the edge of hysteria, but she couldn't control herself. Her temper, when unleashed, was deadly, and Damien had it coming to him. "It took me a while, but I finally figured out why you fly back to New York every three weeks."

"You did, huh? This should be interesting. Go on then, enlighten me."

"You have a girlfriend, or maybe even a wife and some kids to check in with."

"I don't blame you for thinking the worst of me," he said, after a long silence. "I haven't been up front about my personal life, but I didn't want to say anything until I was sure where our relationship was headed."

Through the kitchen window, Marietta announced that lunch was ready.

Damien stepped forward, a tentative smile on his lips. "Come inside and have a bite to eat. We have a lot to discuss, and I'd rather not do it out here. I have the nosiest neighbors."

"Won't *that* be cozy," Niveah spat, convinced he'd taken leave of his senses. "You sitting in between your two lovers, like the player extraordinaire that you are."

"I don't believe in dogging women out, and the last thing I'd ever do is hurt someone I love."

"I'd rather have dental work than sit down and eat lunch with you and—"

Damien seized her arm. "I've had just about enough of your mouth for one day," he grumbled, strolling across the freshly cut lawn.

In the hopes of getting away, Niveah twisted and turned her arm. After several failed attempts, she gave up. It would be easier to free herself from handcuffs than his fierce grip. "Whether you like it or not, we're resolving this issue right now."

The kitchen table was set with clean linens, and the tantalizing aromas drifting around the room instantly made Niveah hungry. Damien led her down a narrow hallway and into a room filled with large windows and furniture that looked contemporary but comfortable.

"Pops, are you ready for lunch?"

It wasn't until Damien released Niveah's hand that she saw the elderly black man in the wheelchair. Deep wrinkles lined his gaunt face, but there was no doubt in her mind who he was. Like his son, Mr. Hunter had chiseled features, broad shoulders and long limbs.

"Marietta made your favorite today, Dad. Minestrone soup, cucumber sandwiches and strawberry pudding for dessert. Doesn't that sound good?"

Mr. Hunter grunted, then shifted around in his chair, as though he was trying to free himself from a straitjacket. "I'm not hungry yet." His voice was gruff and his speech was slightly slurred. "Now get out of here and leave me alone."

Niveah watched Damien bend down and retie the laces on his dad's white tennis shoes. Feeling like an intruder, she turned away, instead choosing to study the framed pictures that lined the sable-brown walls. There were hundreds of photographs of Damien and his father—clowning around in the pool, posing in front of famous monuments, at various sporting events.

"Dad, there's someone here I'd like you to meet."

At the sound of her name, Niveah turned away from the

wall and swallowed the lump in her throat. Wearing her best smile, she stepped forward and said, "It's a pleasure meeting you, sir."

The man nodded but didn't speak.

"Niveah and I have been seeing each other for quite some time," Damien explained, looking up at his dad and resting a hand on his leg. "She's mad at me, Pops, and I was hoping you could help me smooth things over."

His father cracked a smile. "How much you payin', boy?"

"I haven't given it much thought, but I'm sure we can work something out."

"I'm chargin' fifty dollars an hour, and I won't take a penny less!"

Father and son laughed.

"Enough fooling around you two, it's time to eat." Marietta blew into the living room, gripped the handles on Mr. Hunter's wheelchair, and maneuvered it around the coffee table. "I hope you're hungry, because I made you…"

Niveah watched the pair leave, overwhelmed by feelings of pain and sadness. "Damien, why didn't you tell me your dad was sick?"

Damien gestured to the sofa and waited until she sat down before he spoke. "Like I said before, I wanted to see how things played out between us before I said anything. My dad was diagnosed with Huntington's disease almost a year ago, but most of our relatives still don't know. That's the main reason why I left New York. He told me he was doing fine, but I had to come down here to see for myself."

Guilt slammed into Niveah's chest with the force of a battering ram. "Damien, I am so sorry." She couldn't get the words out fast enough. "All this time I thought you were running around with other women and flying to New York every month to be with someone else."

"You were right about that part."

"I was?"

"My parents separated two years ago, and they haven't spoken or seen each other since. My dad moved out here once he started getting sick, and my mom stayed in the city. I've been trying to patch things up between them, but nothing seems to be working."

"Does your mom know that your dad is sick?"

Damien shook his head. "No, and he doesn't want me to tell her, either. He said he wants her to come back because she loves him, not because of pity."

"He's a proud man."

"Now you see where I get it from."

His smile was sad, filled with such anguish that Niveah had to choke down a sob.

"I know I should have told you sooner about my personal problems, but—"

"Damien, you don't owe me an explanation," she said, interrupting. "I understand why you didn't tell me about your father's condition sooner." Moving closer, she placed her hands on his leg and offered what she hoped was seen as gesture of support. "How is his health, overall?"

"He's taking medication to help manage his symptoms, but there's nothing the doctors can do to prevent his physical decline. It's been tough seeing my dad, who's always been in amazing health, become so frail and weak," he explained, lowering his head. "Aside from suffering from severe bouts of depression, he has tremors and trouble walking on his own. That's why I hired a full-time, live-in nurse to help me take care of him. When Mrs. De La Cruz needs the weekend off, her granddaughter, Marietta, fills in."

Niveah sank deeper into the couch. "Oh, I thought… I feel terrible for the way I acted."

"Don't—everyone loses their cool from time to time." Damien cracked a small smile. "Sometimes love brings out the worst in people, and when I saw you talking to Kenyon

Blake at the S.W.A.G. photo shoot I wanted to rip him to shreds!"

He gathered her to him. "I love you, Niveah, and I want to spend the rest of my life with you, but I'm not going to desert my father."

His words stunned her. Niveah sat up, and blinked back tears. "Why would you even say something like that, Damien? I would never ask you to choose between me and your family."

"I'm just making sure. My last relationship ended because my ex hated the idea of my father living with us. She insisted I put him in a nursing home, and when I refused she dumped me. After what happened with her, I'd reconciled myself to living alone, but then I met you and realized that you were a good woman."

Niveah could tell that he wanted to say more. "But?"

"The only thing that's been holding me back from proposing is your insane devotion to your job." His tone softened. "When you choose working over spending time with me, it makes me question whether or not we have a future."

"Damien, advertising has been my life for the last decade, and it's all I know," she confessed. "You've helped to remind me what matters most in life, and it's not promotions or expense accounts. It's family. And learning what you've done for your father makes me admire you even more. I love you, Damien, and I'd be proud to be your wife."

Niveah raised her head, and tasted her lips. The kiss was filled with loving tenderness, but when he pulled away, she sensed that something was wrong.

"There's just one other thing I have to tell you." Resting his arms on his knees, he stared out the side window, his face and arms taut with tension. The light in his eyes, which had been there just seconds ago, was now gone. "I had genetic testing done earlier this year to see if I carry the gene for Huntington disease, and they called me yesterday with the results."

Struck by fear, her breaths came in short, jagged gasps. *No! No! No! God, please no!*

"I'm a carrier, Niveah, which means there's a fifty percent chance that my children will have the disease that's killing my father."

Chapter 17

A fashionable place for professionals, The Ocean Bistro was known for its tasty meals, eclectic decor and spectacular view. Niveah searched the patio area for her friends. Roxi and Jeanette were sitting under a terra-cotta umbrella, laughing all over themselves.

"Sorry I'm late," Niveah said, sliding into the booth. "The next round of drinks is on me."

"What took you so long? We've been waiting for over an hour." Roxi grabbed her fork and held it up like a weapon. "And if you say you were at work, I swear I'll stab you."

Jeanette laughed. "Relax, Kojak. I told you she was with Damien, remember?"

"Oops, I forgot. Guess I better slow down on the mai tais, huh?"

The waitress arrived, set down another round of cocktails and left.

"Well, don't keep me in suspense," Roxi said, turning

toward Niveah. "What's going on with you and dark chocolate? Are you two still doing the nasty?"

Jeanette glanced around the patio. "Must you be so crass?" she hissed.

"Girl, please, I'm from East L.A. Where I come from, people don't mince words."

"I guess it's true what they say, after all—you can take the girl out of the hood, but you can't take the hood out of the girl!"

The women cracked up.

"Damien and I had a long talk this afternoon, and what he told me blew me away," Niveah began, sighing heavily. "The real reason he moved to Tampa was so that he could take care of his ailing father. The VP position had nothing to do with his decision to leave New York, and he doesn't care one way or another if he gets the job."

Her girlfriends listened intently, their eyes wide with interest and concern.

"Wow, that's some heavy stuff." Jeanette blew out a deep breath. "I can't imagine what Damien's going through. Seeing someone you love slowly slip away has to be heartbreaking."

Niveah started to tell her friends about his genetic testing results, but quickly changed her mind. It was private, something he'd shared with her in confidence, and she didn't want to betray his trust. Besides, his test results didn't matter. They'd weather the storms of life—together—just like her parents had back in the day. "I can't believe how well he's handling everything. I'd be a wreck if I were him. A live-in nurse helps him to take care of his dad, but it can't be easy."

"Are you seriously considering settling down with him? I'm not trying to rain on your parade, but someone here has to be the voice of reason. Damien doesn't strike me as the monogamous type, and I wouldn't be surprised if he had another chick on the side."

"Roxi, you're the one who encouraged me to give him a chance, and now you're—"

"Hey, I told you to bang the guy, not fall in love," she said, interrupting. "Niveah, if I were you I'd focus on advancing my career. You've worked too long and too damn hard to throw it all away now. Forget love. Love doesn't pay the bills."

Jeanette made an obscene noise in the back of her throat. It sounded like she was gurgling salt water, and the racket drew the attention of diners sitting at the tables nearby. "Don't listen to her. She's just bitter because Cedrick dumped her last night."

"No, *I* dropped *him*."

"Sure you did, and you gave Niveah your Oprah tickets out of the goodness of your heart, too, right?" Jeanette rolled her eyes. "Now, back to the matter at hand. I'm not going to lie, Niveah. In the beginning, I thought Damien was a player, too, but after seeing you guys together my opinion changed. The man's crazy in love with you, and he's a hundred percent committed to your relationship."

"I don't mean to be insensitive, girl, but do you really want to help Damien care for his sick dad? That's a stress you just don't need. You have a demanding career as it is."

"With that kind of attitude, it's no wonder your ass is alone." Disgusted, Jeanette turned back to Niveah. "Do what feels right and what will ultimately make you happy, because at the end of the day that's all that matters."

"I love Damien and I want to marry him, but there's just one thing holding me back, and it has nothing to do with his father's health."

Roxi frowned. "What is it? Is it about Stewart dumping you on the eve of your wedding?"

"Hell no! I haven't thought about that loser in months." Laughing momentarily lightened Niveah's mood, but her doubts returned seconds later. "I'm worried that I won't be able to juggle a relationship *and* my career."

Jeanette spoke up. "Niveah, it doesn't have to be all or nothing. Look at Mrs. Garrett-Reed. She has a family and a great job. And, sweetie, you can, too."

"I know that in theory, but I've never been able to successfully manage both. Damien's been through a lot this year, and I don't want to end up hurting him. I want to be with him more than anything, but—"

"More than the VP position?" Roxi raised a brow. "Because I'd find that hard to believe."

Niveah wore a smile, one that got brighter as images of Damien and all the special times they'd shared filled her mind. "It's funny, because if you had asked me that question a few months ago, I would have chosen the job. My parents' visit and meeting Damien's father helped me put everything in perspective. I'll be okay, whether or not I'm named vice president. I have a terrific family, a career I'm proud of and I'm dating a guy I absolutely adore. I can't ask for much more than that."

Jeanette flung her arms around Niveah and rocked her from side to side. "This is the best news ever! I'm so happy for you!"

"Well, I'll be damned." Roxi slumped against the booth as if she'd been kicked in the chest. "Niveah-work-means-everything-to-me-Evans has finally found herself a man!"

"Go right in, Ms. Evans. The executive committee will see you now."

Nodding at the receptionist, Niveah strode down the hallway on shaky legs. She was hot and cold, scared and excited, hopeful and anxious all at the same time. This was it. The moment she'd been waiting for all year.

Before opening the door to her boss's office, Niveah took a deep breath and adjusted her cranberry-colored Christian Dior suit. *You can do this,* she told herself, ignoring the knot in the middle of the chest. *You have nothing to worry about. You've got the job in the bag!*

Five middle-aged men clad in dark suits sat around the table speaking in hushed tones. All conversation stopped when she entered the room. The oriental-themed paintings and the gentle sound of water cascading from the marble stone structure created a serene mood, but Niveah was still nervous.

"Please, have a seat," Mr. Russo said, indicating the chair to his left. "We know how busy you are, preparing for the upcoming S.W.A.G. launch, so we'll keep this brief."

The chief financial officer adjusted his tacky red bowtie as if it was choking him. And that's when Niveah knew that she didn't get the job. Relief and disappointment filled her in equal measures. Being passed over for the position made her feel insignificant, like all the hard work she'd done over the last decade had been in vain. On the other hand, now she didn't have to worry about her career getting in the way of her relationship with Damien. Recalling what he'd said to her when he called that morning made Niveah smile.

"Go in there and knock them dead," he'd admonished, the deep timbre of his tone undeniably sexy. "And regardless of what happens today, I'm proud of you, baby."

They hadn't talked more about their future, but she was confident they would, once she returned from her vacation to Chickasaw. Learning about his father's health caused her to see Damien in a new light. He was determined to bring his family back together, and that made her love him even more. She had never felt more secure with a man, never felt more comfortable in her own skin, and she longed for the day when they would be husband and wife. Damien was her Prince Charming, and she refused to let anything come between them. Not her job, not her friends, and certainly not the pain of her past.

"Ms. Evans, we're waiting."

Niveah blinked. Straightening in her chair, she forced her eyes to focus on Mr. Russo. Her boss and his cohorts were staring at her, and each man was wearing an amused expression on his face. Since Niveah had no idea what her boss was waiting for, she said the only thing she could. "I want to thank all of you for considering me for the VP position. Working at Access Media and Entertainment the last ten years has been an amazing experience, and I truly love what I do."

"I think the little lady's in shock." Mr. Russo's comment drew laughs from around the table. He offered her a white manila envelope. "Take a moment to review the contract. We'll wait."

Steadying her shaking hands, she slid the documents out of the envelope and read the cover page. "You want *me* to be vice president?"

Mr. Russo wore a broad grin. "I told you guys she was shocked!"

More hearty chuckles from the peanut gallery.

"Since you missed it the first time around, I'll quickly highlight the specifics of the job again." Her boss cleared his throat, then took a drink from his coffee mug. "You would oversee all twelve departments, but only offer your expertise on the most lucrative projects. Your main responsibility will be planning for the future of the agency. Securing new business, attending meetings and schmoozing with clients is an enormous aspect of the job, but with your stellar reputation, I suspect that companies will be seeking *you* out."

Niveah stared at the document in her hands. Her eyes moved over the first page of the contract, but her mind couldn't process any of the information.

"You'd be doing interviews with the press and traveling overseas to strategize with the managers at other international agencies," continued the director-at-large. An overweight man in his sixties, who looked as if he'd been stuffed into his suit, sounded breathless when he spoke. "You're young and attractive and exactly what Access Media and Entertainment needs to freshen its image."

Is that the only reason why they're offering me the job? Because I have the right "look"? she wondered, feeling knots of tension in her stomach. Her reputation was built on hard work, perseverance and excellence, but to the committee she was just a pretty face.

Niveah sat with her hands folded, her legs crossed, listening pensively as the human resource manager outlined further duties of the job. The more he spoke, the harder it was for Niveah to pay attention. She couldn't afford to blow this opportunity, not when she'd worked so hard to get here, but if she accepted the position, where would that leave her and Damien? Could their relationship survive the strain of such a stressful, demanding job?

"We want you to be the face of the company, and to usher in an exciting new wave in design and advertising. You'd essentially be the front person, someone to woo and impress…"

Niveah knew she was better than this, knew that she wouldn't be fulfilled schmoozing with clients all day long, but she wasn't about to tell the executive committee that. Not until she knew exactly what she wanted to do. She had never consulted her parents when making decisions regarding her career, but she suddenly felt the need to talk things over with her mom and dad.

"We're not trying to press you, but we'll need your response in writing by May twentieth."

"But that's only three days away."

Mr. Russo laced his fingers behind his head and leaned back in his chair. "Frankly, I'm surprised that you need any time at all, Ms. Evans. You've been petitioning for the VP position ever since George announced that he was stepping down."

"I know, sir, but I want to ensure that I'm making the best possible decision for myself and the company." Niveah paused to sip from the glass of water in front of her. "I know you are anxious to fill the position, but I'd really appreciate a few more days to think things over."

"That shouldn't be a problem," the department head said. "How much time do you need?"

"A week would be great."

Mr. Russo nodded. "Very well, then. We'll expect your answer on the twenty-seventh."

Rising, Niveah moved around the mahogany table and shook hands with each member of the executive committee. Then she strode out of her boss's office with her head held high, her shoulders arched and a slight bounce in her step.

Chapter 18

The white Marquee tent could comfortably accommodate a hundred people, but because Mrs. Evans had invited everyone she'd ever met, three times as many guests were crammed inside. While the happy couple posed for pictures in front of their three-tier vanilla cake, friends, family and well wishers guzzled down Mint Julep punch and devoured homemade finger foods.

Damien stood at the entrance of the tent, underneath the silver anniversary banner, drinking his second glass of cognac. Assured by Mrs. Evans that Niveah would be attending the party, he'd booked the first flight out of Tampa and tossed some clothes into a suitcase. And as he searched the room for Niveah, he thought about the conversation he'd had with her mother forty-eight hours earlier.

"I know Norma-Jean's given you a hard time, son, but that's just her way. Pretending she didn't care about anyone or anything helped her cope when the kids bullied her back in grade school. Boys teased her because she was flat-chested, girls hated her because she was smart and teachers liked her. My baby just couldn't win," she'd explained, her voice losing its southern warmth. "Niveah's always believed that if she had a lot of money her life would be perfect, but my daughter's chasing an elusive dream. Money doesn't bring happiness, love does. That's why I want you to hang in there. Niveah loves you, son. You just be patient with her."

Lightning crackled and thunder roared in the distance. Damien glanced over his shoulder and stared up at the bleak, gray sky. Low hanging clouds obscured the sun, but guests were too busy drinking, eating and mingling to notice that a summer storm was brewing outside.

"Have you seen Norma-Jean? I walked past her twice and didn't even realize it was her!"

Raising his glass to his mouth, he discreetly eyed the group of men standing to his right.

"Where is she?" the darkest man queried.

"At the bar with her cousins."

Damien scanned the bar. There she was. His girl. His love. The woman he was destined to spend the rest of his life with. Damien went brain dead every time he saw Niveah, and tonight was no exception. Her black, one-shoulder dress showed just enough skin, and her gold gemstone jewelry enhanced her sexy but classy look.

"Norma-Jean might look different, but she has the same stuck-up attitude she had back in the day," complained a stocky man with a dragon tattoo on his neck. "I tried to talk to her, but she wouldn't give me the time of day. *And* I stepped to her with my best lines."

"It sounds like your game's a little rusty, partner."

The men cranked their necks in Damien's direction.

"You think you can do better?" the man in the straw fedora asked.

"Yeah, but you don't have to take my word for it. I'll show you."

The group guffawed and bumped elbows. "All right, tough guy. Show us what you've got!"

"With pleasure. Watch and learn, fellas." Bent on reaching Niveah before she left the bar, Damien weaved his way around the food tables and through the stylishly dressed crowd.

At the other end of the room, Niveah opened her purse, took out her cell phone and checked for missed calls. Surprised that she had no messages from her assistant, she wondered how her department was faring without her. She'd spoken to Jeanette earlier in the day, and remembering their conversation made her laugh. Word had gotten out at that she'd declined the VP position, and when she answered the phone the first thing Jeanette said was, "I'm so glad you turned down the job! Now we can have a double wedding *and* take our maternity leave together!"

Smiling to herself, she sang along with the oldies song the band was playing. Free of deadlines and all of the pressures at work, Niveah felt relaxed for the first time in months. She didn't know what had possessed her to take a month off work, but when she spotted her parents posing for pictures in front of the rum cake, she remembered. Her mom may have talked her into it, but deep down Niveah wanted to come home. To her surprise, her childhood friends and relatives were thrilled to see her, and had been spoiling her since she arrived last week.

"I don't mean to interrupt, but I just had to come over here to compliment you on your dress. You're a stunner, Norma-Jean."

Her cousins *oohed* and *ahhed* like a game show audience.

Niveah turned, saw Damien standing behind her and thought her heart was going to beat out of her chest. The man was simply and utterly gorgeous. He wore his clothes with style, and looked hot in his black, double-breasted suit. Niveah wanted to ask Damien what he was doing in Chickasaw, but decided to play along with his little game. "Thank you. And you are?"

Damien took her hand, raised it to his mouth, and kissed it. "I'm Damien Hunter."

"Niveah Evans. It's a pleasure to meet you. Are you a friend of the couple?"

"Yeah, I'm going to marry their daughter."

Her smile was full of happiness, piercing him like an arrow to the heart. They stood for a moment in absolute silence, staring at each other, completely oblivious to the confused expressions on her cousins' faces. "I know this is going to seem like an odd question, but do you believe in love at first sight?"

A twinkle shimmered in her eyes. "I didn't, but then I saw you."

"Would it be all right if I kissed you?"

"You don't even have to ask."

"Now, make it good, baby. We have an audience." Damien stepped forward, cupped her chin and tasted her moist, cherry-red lips. He drew his hand down her shoulders and along the smooth curve of her hips. "You look like a piece of candy, and you taste good, too."

Niveah gave him another kiss. "Damien, what are you doing here? I thought you were busy working on the men's shaving ad campaign."

"Your parents invited me, so I came. I think they want to show me off to your relatives."

"I don't doubt it. My mom hand-picked you to be her son-in-law the day you met."

"And what about you?"

Niveah gave him a peck on the lips. "Only time will tell."

"I heard you turned down the VP position."

"And I heard you took it. Congratulations."

"It sucks being their second choice, but the executive

committee has agreed to let me do pro bono work for Huntington's Disease of America, and the company's involvement will help raise a ton of money for patient treatment," he explained. "The lucrative signing bonus that comes with the VP position is a nice incentive, too. My goal is for us to have more kids than Terrence Franklin, and from what my sisters tell me, babies aren't cheap!"

Niveah shook her head. "Sorry, but I don't believe in having children out of wedlock."

"I guess that means we're going to have to get married. When's good for you?"

"I don't know yet. You haven't officially proposed, so it's hard for me to say."

"That throws a wrench in my baby-making plan, doesn't it?" His tone was playful, but the expression on his face was serious. "I'm thrilled that I'm the new company VP, but I'm even more excited about what the future holds for us."

"That makes two of us, baby. You've made me a very happy woman." Slanting her head to the right, she stared up at him, a pensive look on her face. "I don't have a problem with you taking the job, but we have to establish some ground rules."

"Ground rules?" His eyes widened in surprise. "All right, let me hear them."

"First off, no working weekends."

Damien smirked. "Right, as if I work seventy hours a week now."

"And, quitting time is at five, not seven."

"I can *definitely* do that."

"And lastly," Niveah tried to keep a straight face, "no more modeling gigs."

"Now you're taking things too far. I live for those projects!"

The couple shared a laugh.

"Oh yeah, and there's one more thing. Marietta has to go. She's a sweet girl, but I've seen the way she looks at you and I don't like it," she confessed, a note of trepidation in her voice. "When Mrs. De La Cruz needs time off, we'll just have to hire a male nurse."

"That won't be necessary."

Niveah jammed her hands on her hips. *"Oh yes it is."*

"Relax, baby, there's no need to get upset. It's all good." Chuckling, he brushed a stray curl off her forehead. "My mom came home last week and she's here to stay."

"Honey, that's great! I know how much you wanted your parents to work things out, and I'm so glad they finally did!"

"My dad has a long road ahead of him, but he'll be okay. He has to be. He's going to be the best man at our wedding."

"Hmmm…" Niveah stared at her fingers. "Nope, nothing. Still don't see a ring."

He leaned against the bar and drew her to him. "I've never shopped for an engagement ring before, so why don't you give me an idea of what you like, so I don't blow it?"

"Damien, I can't tell you what to buy. That would take all the fun out of it."

"Just humor me, okay?"

"I don't have a dream ring or anything, but I love heirloom designs," she admitted, a smile playing on her lips. "The last time I went shopping with Jeanette, I tried on a platinum ring with a unique, ribbon-twist design, and I loved it so much I didn't want to take it off!"

"I heard about that."

"You should have seen it, baby, it had—"

"Is this it?" Damien raised his right hand and Niveah gasped. He was holding *the* ring. Small, delicate stones adorned the sides of the six-carat diamond, and like that fateful day in the store, seeing it left Niveah breathless.

"Six months ago, you approached me at the Ritz-Carlton bar, and although I acted cool and unfazed, the truth is, I'd been standing there for almost an hour trying to build up the courage to approach you. My nerves prevented me from stepping to you on New Year's Eve, but tonight I'm ready to make the ultimate commitment."

Excitement fluttered in Niveah's stomach. She'd been dreaming of this day for months, but never imagined her wildest dreams would come true tonight.

"Meeting you has been one of the best things to ever happen to me, baby. I've never had someone in my life that I could trust and rely on, and I'm grateful to have you in my corner."

Niveah heard someone sniffling behind her. That's when she noticed all the activity around the room had stopped. The singers stood motionless on the stage, and everyone from the emcee to the banquet servers was watching them. A crowd had gathered around the makeshift bar, and although Niveah couldn't see her mother, she could hear her offering words of encouragement.

"You're my everything, Niveah. You helped me see the good in life when I didn't think there was any, and—" Distracted by a loud noise at the back of the room, Damien lost his train of thought and broke off speaking.

"Go on," she whispered, squeezing his hands. "You're doing great, baby."

Damien lowered his head and brushed his lips across her mouth. "I promise, from this day forward, and for the rest of out lives, to treat you like the jewel you are. Marry me, Niveah and you'll have the love and security that you've always wanted. You'll never want for anything, or ever have to question the way I feel about you."

Niveah started to speak, but her female relatives drowned her out.

"Honey, if she won't marry you, I will!" someone shouted behind her.

"Say yes, girl! He's fine!"

"And gainfully employed, too!" another added.

"I need you in my life," Damien continued, "so marry me and let's have some babies!"

"Of course she'll marry you, son!" Mrs. Evans burst through the crowd, waving her hands wildly in the air like an opera conductor. "And everyone here is invited to the wedding!"

A round of cheers went up.

Dizzy with glee, Niveah laid soft butterfly kisses across Damien's cheeks, nose and lips. He leaned in, got closer. She felt his warmth vibrating through her, felt his undying love in his sweet, tender kiss. Passion built quickly. Exploring his mouth with her tongue increased Niveah's desire. She didn't care that everyone was watching or that her mother had just invited the whole town to her wedding. All that mattered was that she'd found her soul mate, her one and only, and there was no where else she'd rather be than cradled in Damien's strong arms.

Epilogue

One year later

"**S**weetie, you're stunning!" Roxi gushed when Niveah sailed into the living room of her Ritz-Carlton suite wearing a sleeveless white gown embellished with hundreds of pearls. "I've been to a lot of weddings, but I've never seen a more beautiful bride."

"This is nothing. You should see the red Valentino dress she's wearing to the reception," Mrs. Evans said, trailing behind her daughter. "I burst into tears the first time I saw it!"

Jam-packed with bridesmaids, flower girls and a host of female relatives, Niveah's oceanfront suite felt as crowded as a subway platform, and as stiflingly hot. Fanning her face, she walked carefully across the room to where her makeup artist was waiting. With the help of her maid of honor, she sat down in front of the mirror on the tall wooden stool.

"I wonder what surprises Damien has in store for you

today," Jeanette said, smoothing a hand over the front of her gold, strapless gown. "It's going to be hard for him to top what he's already done, but I bet he has something really big planned for the ceremony."

"I almost fainted when I saw that yacht pull up to the dock on Thursday afternoon," a bridesmaid confessed. "I couldn't believe that's where we were having the engagement party."

Roxi agreed. "That was pretty cool, but the fireworks display at the end of the rehearsal dinner was out of this world! I've never seen anything like it."

"Oh, and let's not forget about the food." Aunt Charlotte opened the minibar and swiped a Swiss chocolate bar. "I'm still not sure what caviar and foie gras are, but they're delicious!"

"How are you holding up, pumpkin?" Mrs. Evans picked up the crystal flute on the end table. "Would you like a glass of wine?"

"Wine? Mom, it's only ten-thirty!"

"I know, but I'm feeling stressed." Mrs. Evans downed the contents of the glass in one gulp. "Umm, see? I feel better already!"

Niveah watched the hairstylist adjust her tiara, then secure it with invisible bobby pins. "Mom, what do you have to be nervous about? You're not the one reciting your vows in front of five hundred people. I am."

"I can hardly wait for you and Damien to be married. I did well fixin' you up, didn't I?"

Everyone in the room laughed.

"Has anyone seen my shawl?" Roxi asked, tossing items around on the king-size bed. "I could have sworn it was here a minute ago."

Blocking out all of the chatter in the room, Niveah closed her eyes and allowed the sun streaming into the suite through the balcony windows to calm her nerves. Sounds of nature filled the morning air. Seagulls screeched, waves crashed against the shore and the breeze whistled through tall, leafy palm trees.

Slowly, Niveah recited her wedding vows in her head. It was the first time since arriving at Amelia Island that she had taken a moment for herself, and it was long overdue. Three full days of wedding festivities had been tiring but worth it, and they couldn't have picked a better place for their summer nuptials than the secluded island off the coast of Florida. A popular vacation destination for the young and wealthy, Amelia Island was renowned for its powdery white beaches, enviable views and exceptional dining. Long considered the finest resort in the south, the Ritz-Carlton Chateau demonstrated Southern hospitality at its best.

"Ten minutes until showtime, people!"

At the sound of her wedding planner's voice, Niveah laughed. Claudia Jeffries was a ball of energy, but she was also meticulous, organized and worth every penny of her ten-thousand-dollar fee. Elegance and glamour was the theme of their August wedding, and the in-demand event planner had executed their vision for the day to a tee.

"Don't forget to stuff your bras, ladies!" Claudia waved a box of Kleenex in the air. "I won't have you crying all over your custom-made gowns and ruining Kenyon Blake's fabulous, one-of-a-kind wedding pictures!"

The bridal party crowded around Niveah. After hugs, kisses and words of encouragement, the women disappeared out the suite door.

"I almost forgot. Damien asked me to give this to you." Claudia hustled back over to the dresser. "I'll be back for you in three minutes, so enjoy a few quiet minutes alone."

Niveah took the pink envelope from Claudia and ripped it open. For a long moment, she admired the silhouette on the Hallmark card of the couple walking hand in hand along a beach. A ticket fell onto her lap, and when she saw what it was for, a smile fell across her lips. Now, thanks to her fiancé's generosity, she was the proud owner of a luxury box at the St. Petersburg forum.

Inside the card was a personal, hand-written note that said:

> I want to experience all that life has to offer with you by my side. We'll be able to weather the storms, the ups and the downs, because the love we have for each other is as solid as a rock. Just because I'm making an honest woman of you doesn't mean the fun has to stop, but the next time we make love at a hockey game, it won't be in an underground parking lot—it'll be in the privacy of our very own luxury box.
> Your loving groom,
> Damien

Using her fingertips, she cleaned the tears from her eyes. Clutching the card to her chest, she smiled at her reflection in the mirror. This afternoon she would have everything she'd ever wanted, but didn't think was attainable. She was marrying her soul mate, a man who was loyal, dependable and willing to go the extra mile for her. And his love and support meant more to her than he would ever know.

Niveah allowed her mind to drift back in time, as far back as the night she'd met Damien. Remembering the knock-down, drag-out fight they'd had in his office three days later made her laugh out loud. Imagine him calling her a thief!

As she slipped on her high heels, she wondered if her dad had remembered to give Damien his present. The moment she'd seen it in the jewelry store window, displayed boldly in the middle of a large velvet box, she'd known it was the perfect gift for her fiancé.

The telephone rang, and when Niveah picked up the phone and heard Damien's voice flow smoothly over the line, she smiled a big, girly smile. "Hello to you, too," she greeted, wishing he was in her suite with her instead of on the phone. "I was just thinking about you."

"Did you like your gift? I know it's a little unconventional, but—"

"I loved it, Damien. And I agree, making love in our very own luxury box is better than getting down and dirty on the hood of your car."

"I don't know about all that, but I promised your parents I'd take care of you, and that's what I intend to do," Damien vowed, his voice full of conviction. "I know you're on your way downstairs, but I just had to call to thank you for my new watch. I've been coveting the diamond Concord C1 for months. How did you know?"

"I didn't, but it's exactly your style, and I was pretty confident you'd like it."

"And I love the quote you had engraved on the back. 'Our love will last until the end of time and beyond.' That's beautiful, Niveah."

"I meant every word. I love you, and I can't wait to become Mrs. Damien Hunter."

"I'll meet you at the altar, baby. Don't keep me waiting."

Niveah dropped the phone. Gripping the sides of the chair, she rocked on her heels and pushed herself up. Waiting for her event planner to return wasn't an option, she decided, hustling across the suite. She was going to see the man she loved, and she was going to see him now.

As Niveah stepped out into the hallway, she spotted Claudia speed-walking toward her.

"Great timing. I was just coming to get you," she said, her tone breathless. Moving swifter than a Secret Service agent, Claudia ushered her down the hall and into the private elevator. Within minutes, Niveah was standing outside the lobby of The Crystal Ballroom.

"You're a vision, baby girl. The most beautiful bride to

ever come out of Chickasaw." Mr. Evans gave his daughter a hug. "Are you ready to do this?"

Scared the tears would flow if she tried to speak, she nodded, looped her arm through his, and walked slowly around the corner. "Oh my goodness," escaped from Niveah's lips when she stepped into the ballroom. She knew that Claudia Jeffries was the best wedding planner in the business, but the grandiose decorations blew her away.

The air smelled sweet and was filled with the dizzying fragrance of hundreds of seasonal flowers. Waist-high vases, overflowing with roses, tulips and cherry blossoms, were positioned at both ends of the aisle. Gold tulle beautified the walls and each satin-draped chair was tied with an enormous white bow. Sunlight flowed into the grand ballroom through the domed, stained-glass ceiling, and vintage chandeliers enhanced the romantic ambiance.

Each step Niveah took brought her closer to her destiny. And when she saw Damien standing on the stage her heart swelled with unspeakable happiness. She could sense his excitement, even from twenty feet away, and she increased her pace.

The grand ballroom was filled with family, friends and celebrities, but Niveah couldn't take her eyes off of Damien. He was the most beautiful man she had ever seen, and his smile, all broad and sexy, excited her. The sexual energy pulsing between them was tangible, potent, as real as her drumming heartbeat. And if not for her dad, she would have hiked up her dress and sprinted down the aisle into her fiancé's arms.

Damien stood perfectly still, but inside he was wrestling with his conscience. The event planner had given him strict instructions. He wasn't supposed to move until Niveah crossed the first row of chairs. But as he watched his glowing, resplendent bride move gracefully down the aisle, something powerful came over him. Something he couldn't control. It was as if some unseen force was pushing him across the stage, down the steps and out into the aisle.

The audience gasped.

Damien knew that he was breaking tradition, but he couldn't fight his feelings anymore. His whole body ached to touch her, to kiss her, to hold her. "Thanks for taking a chance on me," he whispered, cradling her face in his palms. "You're my heart and soul and there isn't anything I wouldn't do for you."

"Damien, you are, and always will be, the only man I love."

He stared deep into her eyes, at the woman he cherished and desired so much. This was their time, their moment, the beginning of the rest of their lives. He gathered her to him, and swept his lips across her mouth. And to Damien's joy, she kissed him back.

"Groomsmen, don't just stand there!" the solemn-faced reverend yelled. "Stop them! They can't kiss before I pronounce them husband and wife! That's just not how things are done!"

It took ten minutes and four members of the bridal party to separate the kissing couple. Order was quickly restored and the ceremony continued. Vows were recited, unity candles were lit and diamond rings were exchanged.

Seated at the corner table on the stage, Damien watched as Niveah picked up the pen and signed the marriage license. He nodded at Claudia, who was standing to his left, and then wrapped his arms around his glowing bride.

"Count on me through thick and thin, a friendship that will never end.

When you are weak I will be strong, helping you to carry on.

Call on me, I will be there. Don't be afraid.

Please believe me when I say, count on me…"

Niveah cupped her hands over her mouth. A full gospel choir decked out in gold-and-black robes, sang with one voice. Wearing jubilant expressions, they moved from side to side, signing each word smoothly with their hands. "This is the same choir from Gospel Fest!" she exclaimed, turning toward her new husband. "Damien, this is the best surprise yet."

"If you think this is good, wait until you see what I have planned for the wedding night!" Grinning broadly, he nuzzled his chin against her cheek. "I feel so fortunate to have you in my life. Your happiness is all that matters to me, and I promise to love and cherish you forever."

"I love you, too," Niveah whispered, smiling through her tears, "and when we get to our honeymoon suite, *I* have a secret to share of my own!"

* * * * *

REQUEST YOUR FREE BOOKS!

2 FREE NOVELS
PLUS 2 FREE GIFTS!

KIMANI™
ROMANCE

Love's ultimate destination!

KROM11

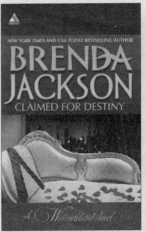

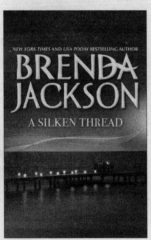